Execution of George Napoleon Woods, 23 June 1882, Durango, Colorado.
Courtesy, La Plata County Hostorical Society.

Knight Errant

The Undoing of George Woods

J. S. Peters

iUniverse, Inc.
Bloomington

Knight Errant
The Undoing of George Woods

iUniverse books may be ordered through booksellers or by contacting:

iUniverse
1663 Liberty Drive
Bloomington, IN 47403
www.iuniverse.com
1-800-Authors (1-800-288-4677)

ISBN: 978-1-4401-7327-1 (sc)
ISBN: 978-1-4401-7329-5 (hc)
ISBN: 978-1-4401-7328-8 (ebk)

Printed in the United States of America

iUniverse rev. date: 05/18/2012

Other Books by the Author

MACE BOWMAN: Texas Feudist, Western Lawman
(With Chuck Parsons)

ROBERT CLAY ALLISON: Requiesat in Pace

HEADLESS IN TAOS: The Dark Fated Tale of Arthur Rockford Manby

Avis Redbird

"There were two sisters sat in a bour;

There came a knight to be their wooer,"

- Anon.

PROLOGUE

George Napoleon Woods scanned the milling crowd before him from the platform of his scaffold. He was the main event in Durango's first legal hanging, and very few wanted to miss the performance. The gallows was erected toward the south end of town on Main, in a weedy and rock-strewn field which sloped gently upward from the street. It was not quite 10 a.m., and although the late Friday morning air lay crisp over the mountain community, the sun in the bright turquoise sky promised a warm June day. The three hundred or so spectators drifted about for what was to them a holiday affair. Children playfully and merrily chased dogs or each other in a game of tag, scampering noisily between wagons and adults. Several clusters of gapers eyed the scaffold while munching sandwiches or slugging down a beer from picnic baskets. In the main they exuded the atmosphere of neighbors gathering for an annual community clambake, swapping recipes, exchanging gossip, trading opinions.

From his elevated vantage point, Woods could see four boys sitting in a row on a large flat boulder on the high ground just beyond the gathering. Severely pressed against each other beneath their cowboy hats, they reminded him of four roosting vultures braced in silent salivation. Between them and the crowd he glimpsed a man in a white starched shirt, dark trousers and dark hat standing frozen, a doll-like young child dressed in her Sunday best anxiously gripping his hand.

He wondered how he would feel as a spectator, whether somehow he could exchange places with someone; remove his shackles, step to the ground, join the observers. Then his eyes caught whom he had sought, the diminutive Emily Stockton, standing on a rock for a better view. On the ground before her stood her half-sister Ellen Stockton and her fiancé, Nathaniel Coldwell. Near them in one of the parked wagons sat Emily's brother John Cowan and his teenaged offsprings, Bill and Lizzie.

At the sight of Emily his heart gave a bounding leap and from his throat came a primal moan, being still a helpless captive of the elixir of romance. He was overwhelmed with embarrassment and agony, the embarrassment of having the woman he loved see him die like a dog at the end of a rope, and the agony that perhaps she too looked upon him as merely the star of a dark celebration. He wished he could fly to her side a moment for just one word, a brief embrace, a farewell kiss. While his emotions were tremulous and turbulent his brain was yet unable to grasp the reality of his actions a month earlier, the act which brought him to this noose. He had the sensation of being detached, alien to what was taking place, puzzled as to why they were doing this to him.

Although it was the killing of exactly four weeks before which delivered him to this scaffold, it all actually began eighteen months previous, upon his first sight of Emily Stockton.

ONE

The very first moment George Woods lay eyes upon Emily Jane Stockton she literally stunned him. The twenty-nine-year-old woman was tiny, alluring and captivating, and the force of her spell left her thirty-year-old admirer moonstruck as a teenager. The perpetual seesaw between his tormenting desire for her and the fear of rejection left him much of the time in a black angst. To compound his dilemma, Emily was a married woman. Add further, her husband was William Porter Stockton, the notorious short-tempered killer of many notches and few words. Usually referred to as a walking obituary notice, he was rumored to have slain eighteen men. He was also the town marshal.

Port Stockton had arrived in Animas City, Colorado three months previously from Cimarron, New Mexico. Few knew that the twenty-nine-year-old Stockton was fleeing four shootings and two murder warrants. Thus his appointment as a man to uphold the law was a sadistic deputation by any standard, a disingenuous cruelty foisted upon an unwary populace. Ike, his younger brother by nearly two years, had already been in the area a year. Having a more people-friendly disposition and wise enough to promote himself as such, he had manipulated Port's position as the town's lawman. Port's position would help cover their rustling activities. As marshal he would keep an eye on things in town while Ike would be the field man between there and New Mexico, across the line where he and some of the gang lived.

Normally it was a trial merely to be in Port's presence, his temperament being so hot and unpredictable. So naturally Woods in his lovelorn state was extra nervous when around him, wondering if Port suspected how he felt about Emily. Not that she and George had ever consummated their relationship, if it could be called one in the first place. She knew absolutely nothing about Woods' moon-struck enchantment, for she had seen and spoken to him but four times since she and Port arrived in town.

Woods was a part-time member of Ike's gang, joining mostly to earn a few well-needed extra dollars in between his regular job as a transient cowboy and some-time carpenter in both Colorado and New Mexico. Consequently in his peregrinations north and south of the state line he became quite familiar with the areas, and in turn a valuable asset to the cattle-collecting group, gaining a knowledge of the trails and herd movements as well as the herdsmen. But what made it more complicated for him was that Port had taken an instant liking to him, and trusted him implicitly. George felt so much safer when he could keep an arm's length from him, but for some odd twist of fate Stockton took to him like a tired foot to a warm sock. "Yessiree, George, ol' buddy," he often enthused. "You're the only friend I got." In sardonic laughter he would add, "Next to my horse and Ike and Emily, that is." But Port's qualifying remarks failed to add any comfort to Woods' already standing-on-thin-ice apprehension. Worse, he was unable to make the intelligent decision of disentangling himself from the potential disaster of a loosened, homicidal Stockton.

In a state of swirling emotional chaos he sat astride his roan before Bill Valliant's Saloon in dusty, hot Animas City. A few other mounts were tied at the rack, and among them he recognized marshal Stockton's. At the sight of the black steed he burst into an uncontrollable fit of trembling and sweat. He wished he had the strength and courage to ride off, but could not. If he made it too obvious that he was avoiding Stockton, questions would be raised, and he could not risk making Port suspicious or angry for any reason, even over a silly thing like shunning him. He had become a mouse drawn to a cobra, a third-rate gambler drawing to an inside straight. He dismounted heavily with a groan and slunk toward the batwing doors, ready to fall upon his six-gun. As he entered the room he desperately pleaded to whatever gods there be that Port would not smell the odor of lust and betrayal he felt certain exuded from his body. The four men at the bar looked his way.

"Hey, George ol' buddy!" hailed Stockton. "Get on over here. Where the hell you been?"

Woods, pale and trembling, waved a paw in half-salute with a crooked half-grin and lied, "Sleeping off a terrible hangover, Port. 'Fraid I can't drink as long and stout as you boys."

"What'd I tell you, Port," laughed fat Milt Buchanan sarcastically. "That child can't drink with us men!"

Woods actually had been riding the hills the past four hours trying to gain a semblance of emotional sanity and balance. But instead he ended up day-dreaming of Emily stronger than ever. The ride itself had drawn him further in his need for her, instead of clearing his mind as he hoped it would. The verdant forest, whirring birds, occasional skittering rabbits or deer, the natural rich panorama of nature sucked him deeper into the unconscious primal force which fed his fantasy-wracked brain. It fortified his romantic notions instead of flushing his heart with the intelligence he desired, and he was left more drugged than before, more eager for whatever colorful visions his imagination could conjure up so as to aid him in breeching the walls of reality.

"C'mon, George," invited Stockton. "What you need is some hair of the dog. Pour the man a double, Valliant. It's on me."

"Thanks, Port," replied Woods as he quickly grabbed the glass with a shaking hand and sweat-beaded forehead.

"My god, George," amazed Dyson Eskridge. "You must be in real terrible shape, with the trembles as bad as that."

"And you got the sweats, too," added Harg, Dyson's brother. "Maybe you got some kind of flu?"

"No, no," returned Woods quickly and defensively. "Just got to get something to eat and I'll be o. k."

"Hell, George," commented Valliant. "I got a pot of stew in the back. I'll get you some."

Before Woods could protest, being neither hungry nor hung over, Valliant left. Woods then thought to let things go as it were. After all, they gave him all the cover he needed for his counterfeit hangover condition.

Suety Milt Buchanan grumbled again, somewhat snottily, "What's all the fuss over a pussy that can't drink? Feed him a bucket of milk and be done with it, for Christ's sake!"

Woods had the blackest desire to draw his Colt and pistol-whip the obese man's head to a pulp right then and there. As he was preparing to give an insulting retort as an introduction to the deed, Port interjected icily, "Big fat fuckin Milt, shut up. Leave friend George be."

"O. k., o. k., o. k.,"whined Buchanan, backtracking. "Just joshing, Port, that's all, honest."

For some unfathomable reason Milt took an immediate dislike for Woods the first they met, and rode him ever since. Perhaps it was the limited intelligence of a bully who can smell someone he can push about. A primal jungle thing. Not that Woods wouldn't fight, but it was just that it was the last-resort behavior in his make-up. And not being physically aggressive nor having a warrior's mentality, he would rather walk than fight. He had won and lost his share of altercations of the few he had had, and also had seen the outcome of the physical slaughter some losers absorbed, a few of whom died, and saw no sense to it. Buchanan seemed to have sniffed all this and in his sage misinterpretations gloried in his ceaseless badgering.

"Here you are, George," invited Bill Valliant as he sat a huge steaming bowl of buffalo stew and a stack of warm tortillas before him. "Get healthy, ol' buddy."

"Lord, thanks Bill. Really kind of you."

The rich aroma of buffalo meat smothered in potatoes and vegetables gripped Woods' stomach. Not having eaten a solid meal for two days because of his brooding he dug in heartily before his amused audience. Obese Milt Buchanan sat in seething silence, jealous of his target's attention. But he was not a complete idiot, so bit his tongue. He knew first-hand of Stockton's murderous rages, and remembered witnessing the near-death experience of a local citizen shortly after Port pinned on his badge.

Two months before, in July, mercantile man and future mayor George Kephart appeared on the street with a revolver in his waistband. Animas City had an ordinance prohibiting carrying firearms within city limits and Port righteously enforced it, but he was motivated more for his share of the fines than its legal imposition. Stockton approached him and demanded the weapon.

"Oh, good heavens, marshal!"came Kephart's embarrassed laugh. "I absentmindedly forgot it was stuck in my trousers. Please excuse me, but I just stepped out of my shop to go to the drugstore. I'll return to my place right now and leave it."

"No, you'll just hand it over to me right now and be fined like anyone else."

"But, surely, marshal . . . ."

"I said hand the damn thing over!"

"Now, marshal, don't you think you're being a little unreasonable?"

"You damn idjit!" fumed the law, as he grabbed and withdrew the merchant's gun from his waist. "I said *gimmie!*"

Kephart clasped a hand around Stockton's wrist and tried to push him away. Twisting, cursing and snarling, Port then drew his Colt with his free hand. Kephart clamped that wrist too, and the two became locked in a scuffle in the middle of the street, looking like a pair of ungainly dancers alternately pushing and pulling at each other as they enthusiastically kicked up the dust in a four-handed cowboy polka. The dance came to a sudden stop as the marshal squeezed off a round from his gun which caught the merchant in the jaw. Stunned, Kephart stumbled back a step and sprawled full-length on his back, semi-conscious. Stockton holstered his weapon, jammed the other in his waistband, then leaned curiously over the prone body. "Well? You alive?"

The merchant groaned as he turned on an elbow to cough and spew blood and teeth.

"I hope you're happy now, you damn fool. Guess you know, resisting an officer of the law is an additional fine. People like you are gonna make me rich," he chuckled. "Don't move. I'll go get a doctor." It was then that he saw Buchanan gaping and shaking and pale on the board walk. "What in hell you staring at, fat boy? Ain't you ever seen a man shot up before? Run and get a doctor for this fool pronto, or I'll bounce a bullet off your lardy ass!"

Without a word Buchanan waddled off like an unwieldy whale.

Following the Kephart shooting the town officials wondered seriously over their selected lawman and began to feel caged by their choice. But Stockton, wrapped in the intoxicating power of his new-found authority, felt invigorated, and strut about more cocky than before.

"Well, George," grinned Port as Woods wiped the remains of his bowl with the last piece of tortilla. "Gonna live now?"

"You bet. Bill, that was the best stew I've ever eaten. A true feast for a hungry heart."

"Thanks, George. And you're welcome to a refill if you have the room."

"No, no, I've had all I can handle. But I will have a beer to wash it down with."

"Coming right up."

"Say, Dison," asked Stockton. "Ain't there a new barber in town?"

"Sure is. Some kinda foreigner."

"A nigra, I hear," injected Buchanan deprecatingly.

"Well, I need a shave and guess I'll try him out. Looks like you could use a shave yourself, George. C'mon, treat's on me."

Robot like, Woods trailed after Stockton to the shop next door. Barber J. W. Allen, an aborigine of Australia, was alone. He had taken over that week for the owner who wanted some time off. As the marshal hung his hat on the rack and plopped into the chair, he slid his holster around to his front where it sat between his legs. "I need a shave, nigger," he ordered rudely and gruffly. Woods sat at the far end of the bench, embarrassed, burying his face in an old newspaper.

"Yes, sir, sheriff," returned Allen good-naturedly, snapping the white sheet smartly, then floating it gently and expertly over the lawman.

"Where you from, boy?" grilled Port.

"Australia, sir," he answered with a touch of pride.

"Aus-*TRA*-lia? Where in hell's that?"

"Across the ocean, sir. The Pacific Ocean."

"Damn! How far that be?"

"Over seven thousand miles southwest of San Francisco, sir."

"Hot damn! Big country?"

"Nearly three million square miles. A very vast land, sir."

"Double damn! Must be near big as these United States."

"That it is, sir."

"You got good manners for a nigger, boy."

"Thank you, sir."

"They run many slaves out there?"

"Oh, no, sir. No slaves. Absolutely not."

"But they do have *niggers?*"

"Actually we are called aborigines, sir. We are the original natives of the country. The whites came much later, convicts from England."

"*Abor*-what?"

"Aborigines, sir. Native citizens. Like your American Indian is the aborigine of America. The whites came later, taking the country from them."

"You mean this country ain't mine?"

"Oh, no, sir. What I mean is that this country was originally theirs, but was taken from them by European intruders. The crude right-of-conquest sort of thing."

"So what in hell's wrong with that? If you want something, take it. If someone can't hold onto what's theirs, they don't deserve it."

"A rather primitive concept, sir, if I may be permitted to say so. Civilization could not long survive such savage tenets."

Stockton fixed his ice-blue agates on the barber's deep brown orbs in a flash of disapproval, quickly wrapping his hand around the butt of his covered side-arm with no subterfuge whatsoever.

"You pretty smart for a nigger, know that?"

"You are too kind, sir," replied Allen nervously, unable to tear his eyes away from Port's penetrating stare. It gave him the sensation of sinking into a pit of quicksand, blue quicksand. Attempting to appear unperturbed he scraped at the marshal's jaw humming a melody out of tune.

"In fact," Stockton hissed, "I think you all is just another smart-assed coon."

A sudden, uncontrollable tic ran through Allen's body, causing him to tightly grip his razor out of the fear that he may give vent to his repressed rage. As a result the blade nicked Port's chin.

"*Cut me, will you, nigger?!*" bellowed the marshal in unleashed fury as he leaped from the chair and roughly shoved the barber aside. Wide-eyed and in shock Allen watched in frozen terror as Stockton tried to rid himself of the white apron, cursing insanely as he twisted and flailed about like a great white-winged bat. The lawman finally freed himself and in his excited state got off two shots which shattered the mirror off the wall. He then commenced clubbing the Allen about the head and shoulders with the gun barrel. With a shout the barber fled out the door and down the street in a race for his life. Port was right behind him but the sprinting aborigine was wasting no time, making tracks. Stockton halted and took aim in order to bring him down, getting off two rapid shots before he disappeared around the corner.

One of the slugs slightly pressed his skull, but it merely encouraged him to increase his speed and distance.

Woods emerged from the shop in a stupor, wondering at Port's sanity. The display he witnessed was strictly out of bedlam. Stockton merely grumbled at his poor marksmanship, ejected the spent shells into the street, reloaded and holstered his gun. "Let's go for a drink, George."

They reentered Bill Valliant's Saloon, and as Port downed several bolts of whiskey with side gulps of beer, he was not shy in describing his close brush with death, and went to great lengths in portraying the "crazed, razor-wielding nigger" who tried to take his life, showing off his slightly scrapped chin with its barely discernable trickle of crimson.

"Yessiree, goddamit, I fixed his wagon!" raved Port. "Ain't no nigger alive gonna cut the face of William Porter Stockton! Especially a foreign one!" He downed three more hefty shots and sipped a fourth while alternately working on a third glass of beer. Suddenly downing both in a fury with a "Let's go George!" he stumbled into the glaring sun and clambered aboard his horse. Woods, pale with anxiety, sat his mount and unconvincingly stammered about having some ranch work to do. Stockton glared at him in bleary red-eyed hostility for a very long and tense moment, then turned his horse toward the Animas River bridge aiming toward home. Woods was relieved to see him go.

Suddenly appearing from nowhere came a pair of armed men afoot, one with a shotgun, the other with a Winchester. They were Mayor Gene Engley and the giant blacksmith, Charlie Naegelin.

"Stop where you are, Port," ordered the Mayor. "And get off your horse," he added, emphasizing his request by cranking a shell into his Winchester.

George quietly sidled his mount around the corner, watching from behind some trees.

"What the hell's going on, Engley?" snarled Stockton.

"Barber Allen's told us about your last caper, that's what. And you're through as a lawman in this town, is another."

"*SHE-IT!*" flung Stockton. "You gonna believe a nigger over a white man? And a foreign one at that? What in hell is the world coming to? That sucker threatened to cut my throat. *Looky* here at my jaw where he near slashed me," he emphasized, pulling down on his collar with a grimy finger. "See? It's still bleeding!"

"No more bullshit, Port. Get down off that horse, *now!*"

"Ja, Porter," echoed the hulking smithy. "Do like de Mayor says." He cocked both hammers of his shotgun pointed only yards from the gunman's head.

Red-eyed Stockton wanted in the worse way to draw and drop them both in their tracks, but knew his chances of success were nil, that they had the edge. So he grudgingly dismounted. "Engley, you're making a big mistake. You really are."

"We got particulars on you from Cimarron and Otero this morning," stated the Mayor to the unhorsed ex-lawman. "Like a couple of outstanding warrants. Seems you are too free with your gunpowder. Now unhook your gun belt and hang it over your saddle horn. Slow and careful."

Stockton did as requested, feeling unnaturally unmanned and naked as he turned from his mount to face his captors. "C'mon, Engley, I was only enforcing the law."

"Like you enforced it shooting Kephart in the jaw?"

"Hell, Mayor, he broke city ordinance and gave me a lotta lip, refusing to surrender his gun like he should of. If a citizen don't show no respect for my authority, what else was I to do?"

"Just unpin your badge and hand it over, Port. It hurts my eyes seeing it on you," replied Engley, extending his left hand, his other gripping the stock and trigger of his cocked rifle pointed at Porter's gut.

"O. k, o. k.," he muttered as he did so.

"Consider yourself canned," retorted Engley as he slipped the star into his shirt pocket and relieved Stockton of his reins. "Now walk on ahead of us to the jail."

As the trio moved away Woods silently turned and rode out of town.

"I wish you wouldn't do this Mayor. Just let me go and I'll gladly ride on outta here and never come back. Honest."

"No. Only way you're leaving this town is with the Colfax County Sheriff when he comes to claim you."

Stockton's memory of his last conversation with Sheriff Pete Burleson and deputy Mace Bowman weren't comfortable ones, and they were the last men he cared to see.

The calaboose was a three-celled 14x14 feet log blockhouse with one barred door window. A fourth room was furnished with a potbellied stove, desk and chair for the convenience of a guard. "Engley?" half-pleaded Stockton.

"Yeah?"

"Can I have dinner with my wife tonight?"

"Don't see why not. What time?"

"Tell her at six."

"O.k. We'll take you over and baby-sit you until you're done,"

At a few minutes before six Engley and Naegelin escorted Stockton to his house a few blocks away. At his door the mayor instructed him, "We'll be outside, Port. You got an hour."

Thanks, Mayor," came his acrid retort. "Mighty white of you."

Once inside Stockton wasted no time in his hyperactive state. He sparked his wife, gulped his food, then grabbed his Winchester, spare Colt and a box of 44.40 ammo which fit both weapons.

"Honey, I got to get to gettin' or they'll surely see that I'm sent back to Cimarron, which is the last place I need to be."

"Oh, God, Porter, all this over shooting a damn nigger? What's the world coming to?"

"I know, honey, I know. But try telling them Yankee carpetbaggers that. They keep kissing up to them coons like they were kin, and they most surely are. Next thing you know they going to be shedding tears over taking this country away from them savage Redskins!"

"Oh, Porter, where you going? When will I see you again?"

"Listen, I'm heading down to Ike's place in New Mexico. What I want you to do is get George Woods and tell him to drive you and the young 'uns down there. That's where we'll be living for a time now."

With a hasty hug for his wife and two daughters, Sarah eight, and Mary five, and a peck on the head of year-old Carrie, Stockton quietly exited the cabin out a back window, slipping into the trees and away from his guards. Three blocks away he accosted George West who was casually riding by, unceremoniously yanked him out of the saddle of his lovely horse, then galloped out of town. By the time Engley and Naegelin discovered their blunder, the outlaw had a twenty minute start in his escape. As the two ran toward the law office West was already there waiting and fuming over the loss of his prize horse.

"Damn it, Mayor! Stockton done stole my horse! Pulled me off it and galloped away!"

"I know, I know, don't tell me what I already know! Me and Charlie are going after him right now! Don't worry, we'll get him!"

Engley deputized Naegelin on the spot, and within twenty minutes with pistols, rifles and ammunition the two rode out after Stockton. The smithy was the less enthusiastic and the more realistic of the duo, having merely volunteered in the first place to assist the mayor in apprehending Stockton. His civic duty now over, he looked forward to returning to his shop, his instinct for survival more than satisfied. But now here he was, offering himself as a target by chasing after a hair-triggered, sadistic killer. Naegelin knew Stockton and what a wild-card he was, and if it weren't for the fact that the mayor would again be alone in his pursuit, he would happily surrender his badge immediately. So he nervously stuck with him, hoping the renegade would successfully elude them and escape without so much as a shot.

Miles later they crossed the Florida River in the growing darkness and headed south to Ignacio, near the New Mexico line. Stockton's old Texas friends, the O'Neal family, had a ranch on the edge of the village, and Engley figured he would probably stop for a rest to feed himself and his horse before going on, maybe even spending the night.

"It's getting awful dark, Mayor," observed the smithy. "How long you vant to go after dis bird?"

"He can't be too far ahead. I think he'll most likely stop for awhile at O'Neal's. That's where we'll take him."

O'Neal, thought Naegelin. Another bad apple. "Vell, I hope ve don't come into an ambush, so dark it is."

"Hell, it's just as dark for them, Charlie. We'll be fine."

At the O'Neals the men walked their mounts about, checking the barn and other structures, riding into some of the dense brush and trees, listening, peering into the thick night. It was moonless and spooky-quiet, except for the sounds of their horse's blown breathing and the thumping of the blacksmith's heart. There were no lights from the house, but the mayor alighted and rapped loud enough to shiver and shake the smithy's spine, knowing what targets the two must make. But no one answered. Making another quick tour of the property, Engley threw in the towel, not realizing they were being observed by Stockton and several O'Neals a gunshot away.

"Hell, let's go on back to town, Charlie. He ain't here. He's probably down in New Mexico by now. I guessed wrong."

Tremendously relieved, Naegelin turned his mount and thankfully joined him.

TWO

When Port arrived at Ike's ranch house in the late morning it was a surprise visit he didn't expect. Yet when Ike saw his brother coming in astride a somewhat exhausted steed, a sinking feeling came over him. God damn it, he muttered. Now what? What in hell's he screwed up now? He felt in his bones the day before that something was about to go wrong, and he hoped it weren't bad news. At least not so bad it couldn't be fixed.

Yet he loved Port, he really did, even though much of the time he pissed him off. Always pushing, always in hot water, always seeming to purposefully look for the quickest way to stick his hand in the fire. As he stood in the doorway watching the lone rider approach at a gallop, his five-year-old daughter Delilah excitedly shoved past him in a rushing squeal, "Uncle Port! Uncle Port!"

Port laughed at the sight of her barefooted self kicking up dust, jumping up and down in the yard and squealing like an overwrought puppy. Breaking his mount to a sliding stop he exclaimed, "Good lord, Lelia! You've growed a foot and a half since I last seen you!"

She threw up her arms to him in excitement as Port deftly leaned to snatch her from the ground, wrapping her in one arm as he walked the roan toward Ike on the porch. "And heavenly days, Lelia," he scolded with a grin. "You've also put on pounds I'd be ashamed to admit to!"

Stepping down from the porch Ike grimly took the horse's bit and stroked its head. "This poor beast is a healthy looking mount, but by God I think it's going to drop in its tracks if you don't alight and let me tend to it. Get down and let me take him to the barn 'fore he drops right here."

"Nonsense, Ike," quipped Port. "He's got at least another mile left in him, I guarantee."

"Are you unhinged?" scolded Ike. "All you can guarantee from this blown traveler is dog meat if you don't give it a good rest. And I notice from the brand that it ain't yours. Belongs to George West, I reckon."

"Come to think on it, you're right," he smirked. "Had to borrow it in a hurry."

Ike shook his head in resignation as he led the exhausted roan to the barn while Port carried the happily chattering Delilah into the house.

"That you, Port?" called a female voice from the kitchen.

"Sure is. How you be, Ellen?"

"Fine, just fine."

Twenty-two-year-old Amanda Ellen Robinson had become Ike's wife six years previous in Texas where he had returned following several Lacy-Coleman cattle drives to Colfax County, New Mexico. Port remained behind in Otero, New Mexico with Emily and their first child Sarah, feeling safer maintaining distance between him and Erath County, Texas where he still had an outstanding warrant on him for attempted murder. The two had wed childhood sweethearts, Port first with Emily Cowan, Ike later with Amanda Robinson. Both girls were eight years apart and first cousins to Port and Ike. After Emily's parents demise their six offspring moved in with relatives, John and Sarah Robinson, and their two-year-old granddaughter, Amanda. The two girls bonded and in time gravitated toward the neighborhood boys, Port and Ike. As the years passed the quartet became inseparable companions, then finally married. An older brother of Emily's, John Cowan, had two children, then lost his wife and child to her third birthing. He too moved from Erath County to Colfax County, then to Animas City, John working with Ike as an occasional "herder." It was with John that Port and Emily had been living before Port's barber-whipping caper.

While both girls saw the Stockton men as a way out of a confining and overcrowded family situation, young Ellen was the least happy of the two. Emily clung to Port no matter what he did, whom he slew, or how often they had to move. She loved him with the passion of the true believer, and found his swaggering persona captivating. Ellen's early romantic veneration of Ike folded rather quickly, having a more realistic aim at what she wanted out of life, or for certain what she did not want. Before long she began to feel cheated and short-changed. "I'm sick of Ike's cowboy shit," was her favorite summing up to Emily as she constantly complained. "I want something a hell of lot better than this, having babies and playing cook to a lying, thieving gunman."

"Oh, Ellen, honey," Emily would chide. You're just so unsettled and young. Give Ike a chance. He's trying real hard to get a ranch and a herd together, and I know he'll do it. Port, too. In a little while we'll all be in New Mexico and things'll change. You wait and see!"

"Good God, Emily! How can you believe all that silly talk? Look at you and ugly-tempered Port. He's been killing and running since he almost clubbed his pappy to death on his front porch back in Texas. All you got to show since then is three young 'uns and a handful of warrants. Woman, you might be older than me but I don't think you got a lick of sense!"

"Now you listen here, Ellen. The difference between you and me is that I love Port as I love my own breath, and he loves me as hard. I know you don't love Ike, that he was just a passport out of Texas. Port was my passport too, I don't deny that. But we love each other. That's the real difference and you know it. He might not amount to much dollar-wise, but he treats me and the young 'uns like royalty. Crazy as he might act and temperamental as he may be, he is a lamb at home and as thoughtful as can be to all our needs. I'm just sorry you and Ike drifted apart."

Twenty-two-year-old Ellen gazed at her twenty-nine-year-old friend, wondering where in hell it would all end for them. "Oh, Emily, I'm sorry I bitch all the time about them men. I'm just so damn disgusted and disappointed over how Ike turned out to be in comparison to what he promised and lied about. If he was at least an honest cowman or a hard-working farmer maybe I wouldn't be so unhappy. Oh, hell, I don't know!"

And now Ellen seeing Port galloping up on a sweaty, worn nag all laughs and smiles as if everything was sweet and rosy aggravated her no end. Who in hell did he kill now? And what was he running from again? Seeing Port was like witnessing her own dismal and empty future, and reminding her of her lifeless marriage. Every time she saw him it reinforced her bottomless anger to where she could hardly hold her tongue. The few times she did express her dissatisfaction, Ike, without hesitation or warning instantly swung out backhandedly and sent her sprawling across the floor. After three separate swats in three consecutive days she wisely held her rebellion in check, repressing her opinions, and began to wish for his immediate death in a shootout with the law. But to her chagrin luck was always with him. Yes, she thought to herself, watching Port enter the kitchen, in his cocky swagger which further infuriated her, Ike's cowboy shit was really getting old.

"Come on in, Port," she dryly invited with an automatic smile. "Let me fix you up a breakfast." Oh, how she wished she could cook him up a platter of poison!

With Delilah still in his arms he pranced to the table and sat her in a chair, then took a seat opposite her. "Thank you, yes, I do have a terrible hunger. And give my pard here a big glass of milk."

Out in the barn Ike unsaddled and unbridled the lathered roan and proceeded to gently wipe and rub him down, talking to him soothingly. He pampered the exhausted beast lovingly, giving him a light meal of oats, careful not to let it overeat or over drink. Holding a deep regard for horses, it upset him gravely to see this beautiful specimen so unnecessarily abused. He knew that if Port had had his way the mount would have been long dead. No matter how he tried explaining to his brother how sacred horseflesh was, that it was more than mere transportation, it never sank in. Port just loved to ride them to death, and seemingly spitefully. He recalled how Port had beat their father's prize mare brutally, angrily, and how the poor animal came to tremble bug-eyed at the sight of him.

Good, lord, Ike," came Port's voice from the barn door. "You still pampering that jug of glue?"

"Christ, Port. You never learn, do you?"

"Aw, please, little brother. Not another lecture."

"I wouldn't waste my breath," grunted Ike. "So I guess your lawman days are a thing of the past, right?"

"Sure am. They don't want no law in that burg anyways. I try and enforce ordinances and get laughed at. Then this buck nigger barber tries to take a razor to me. So I smacks him side of the head with my gun and gets fired for my troubles."

"Port, listen a minute, please? Just one minute, o. k.?"

Porter shifted his feet in embarrassment, knowing he wasn't telling the whole truth, and knew Ike was aware of it. "Sure, Ike. Sure."

"Your job as town marshal was important for what I needed. But hell, what's done is done. If I'd had any sense I'd have taken the job myself and let you keep an eye on things down here. As it is, you're right where you should of been in the first place. So let's work with that, all right?"

"Now you're talking. I promise you got nothing to worry about with me down here. I can ram-rod this outfit no problem. I promise you that."

Ike wasn't sure how to answer, or rather, knew how he wanted to answer, Port being such a loose canon, but realized it would end up just another of a series of disagreements and hot quarreling, so just tactfully bit his tongue. Port had grown so testy even a cloudy day could set him off. He was getting worse, like daring the grim reaper to take him away, and if the reaper had any sense he'd leave him alone. His life had become nothing more than a string of murderous displays of temper with not a thought of consequence, care or concern. It had earlier been four years since seeing each other, and he seemed more of a stranger than ever. Back then in Cimarron when Ike broke him out of jail by jamming his gun in the jailer's gut, at least he had a sense of humor, but now even that was gone. Ike left the vicinity right after, knowing the law wouldn't look too kindly on him freeing one of their prisoners so unlegally, moving south to Lincoln County. Ike tried his damnedest to get Port to leave with him, but no, he was determined to stay. No one was going to run him off, so stay he did, blustering and killing a few more times like he was on a holiday. Somehow he miraculously survived. It was the deep fear people had of him, that and the smell of death he gave off, at least in their imaginations.

Port always was like a crazy, unruly kid, the less mature of the two, although nearly two years older. It was as if Ike was forever picking up after an uncontrollable child. At first it was a game, a lark. But slowly it grew to where Ike wanted to put space between them, miles finally, and thankfully. But it came with a measure of guilt for the blood-tie was too deep. In their separations there was no true severance, only the physical measurement of space and miles. They were fated in some manner to close in on their individual futures as if they had a score to settle with destiny. And so, there wasn't a thing Ike wouldn't do for Port if the occasion arose. For instance, there was the time when a trio of thugs pulled a prank on Port that gave Ike the furies, to the point of wanting to ride back to Cimarron to kill all three. And he would have too, but he soon cooled down.

The trio, Davy Crockett, Gus Hefferon and Henry Goodman, were in Lambert's saloon one afternoon when they got the bright idea of setting up a Mexican acquaintance.

"Hey, 'Tonio," greeted Crockett jubilantly. "How in hell are you all doing?"

"Bueno, Davy," smiled Antonio Arcibia. "Muy bueno."

"Well, hell, ol' buddy," enthused Goodman. "Have a couple beers on me!"

"Me too!" echoed Hefferon. "Ain't seen you in a coon's age."

They ordered glasses of beer which were set before Arcibia two and three at a time, and he played hell trying to get them down as soon as they appeared in an effort to keep up with his magnanimous patrons. After Arcibia's ninth or tenth glass his speech and slight weaving were telling, and Crockett leaned over to whisper confidentially, "'Tonio, me and Heff and Henry want to play a joke on an ol' friend. Would you help us, compadre?"

"A joke?"

"Si, hombre," added Hefferon from his other side, sliding a comeradely arm about his shoulders. "A harmless jest. A prank."

"Well, shore," grinned Arcibia. "I guess."

"See that fella at the end of the bar," confided Crockett. "Alone, drinking a beer?"

"Si, I see."

"What we want you to do is walk over to him and say, 'Mister, I want you to keep away from my wife.'"

"Oh, no, Davy. That's too mean! An' I don't even know heem!"

"Aw, c'mon, Antonio," injected Goodman. "We play jokes on each other all the time. It don't mean a thing!"

"Sure, companero," echoed Hefferon laughingly. "Ain't nothing to worry over."

"Senors, I doan know . . ."

"And right after, soon's you tell him that, we'll come over and straighten it all out," soothed Crockett. "O.k.?"

"Weeeell . . ." undecided Arcibia.

"Here, have another beer before you go," urged Hefferon, sliding a full glass before him. "Chug it down. Ain't a thing to fret over. Later we'll tell you somma the stuff he's pulled on us. Lordy, you'll split a gut!"

Antonio downed his beer with machismo gusto, wiped his mouth with his sleeve, ceremoniously tugged down on his sombrero to place it at a cocky angle, and laughed with his three friends. "Hokay, mi companeros," he grinned, as he made his way as businesslike as he could along the bar toward Porter Stockton, who was stonily staring off into space over his beer. There were only two customers at the bar between he and Stockton, and Arcibia unsteadily rolled around them along his way. Two of the six tables were occupied, and a pair of cowboys were playing a friendly game of pool. As Port's peripheral vision caught Antonio weaving toward him, he casually dropped his right hand to his holster and flipped the hammer-thong from the hammer of his Colt.

"Senor," slurred Arcibia in as menacing manner as he could muster. "*Ahem!* Senor!"

Stockton turned his agate-blue orbs on the intruder, observing he was unarmed.

"I want joose to keep from my wife!"

Stockton, puzzled, stared a moment trying to decipher the accusation.

"You hear me? Joose doan unnerstan English?"

The barroom grew quiet as a morgue. The bartender moved to a far corner, trying to make himself smaller and invisible. The cowboy at the pool table who was bent to shoot froze in position, staring over his shoulder at Stockton, wishing he were elsewhere.

"I sed," emphasized Antonio, the alcohol he had imbibed now assisting him to play the role of wronged husband. "I sed, *I wan joose to keep from mi esposa!*"

Stockton drew and put a pair of bullets square into Arcibia's chest as if he were swatting a pesky fly. The impact drove the shocked Antonio back several steps and he fell in a sprawl on his back, dead before he hit the floor.

"Goddam dumb greaser," muttered Stockton, as he cleared the cylinder of the two expended shells. In the dead silence the brass casings hitting the floor clattered echoingly throughout the room, the cordite hanging thick and pungent. With a contemptuous air he slowly reloaded the two empty cylinders, re-holstered the Colt, then drained his glass of beer. Strolling past the deceased, he gave him a shoving nudge with the toe of his boot to make sure he was dead, then walked out.

"Jesus H. Christ!" blew Goodman. "I ain't never ever gonna accuse Port of straying long as I live!"

"Amen," echoed Crockett. "Neither will 'Tonio, I recken!"

"I'll drink to that," grinned Hefferon.

Ike was down in Lincoln County when he heard the whole story and was set to make the journey north to pick up three quick notches, so heated he was over the stupid stunt. Then word came of Crockett and Hefferon being shot off their horses one night by the law. Crockett died, and the wounded Hefferon fled town soon after he broke out of jail, ending up in Durango to join the Stockton-Eskeridge gang. Goodman too showed up in Durango, but moved off to become a successful rancher in Utah. Fortunately, time had tempered Ike's desire for justice.

The irony behind the tragedy was that Port was a man who never strayed or made light of his marriage vows. He and Emily were and always would be crazy about each other, emotionally held tighter than Siamese twins. Thus, when the three Cimarronites talked the unwitting Arcibia to partake of their stunt, they sadistically and knowingly sealed his death warrant. It was an accusation Port saw no humor in, for he saw it not only as an insult to their marriage and an affront to his feelings toward his wife, but as a personal slur on Emily.

"So anyway, Port" continued Ike. "You and Emily take over my place here and we'll move on up to Animas City. Emily and the young 'uns are coming down soon, aren't they?"

"Sure are. They should be here in a day or two. I told her to have George Woods drive them down."

"George? Good man. Highly trustworthy."

"I think so too."

THREE

That very morning, an hour after dawn, George Woods and Emily Stockton left Animas City in a wagon pulled by a pair of mules. Two horses trailed them at the end of secured tethers, one Port's, the other George's. The three girls lay asleep bundled in blankets against the morning chill amid a cluster of goods, and several battered pieces of furniture. Woods was brimming over in a repressed state of enthrallment, wanting and not wanting to pinch himself awake. Here he was at last, alone with the woman he had perpetually fascinated over the past three months. He swore to make the most of the trip, caress each and every minute. But he also knew that he had to be sensible, cautious and guarded in his conversation, for Porter would murder him in a flash at the mere suspicion of his thoughts. Still, one part of him wished to cry out, throw survival to the winds by announcing his love regardless of acceptance or rejection, to free him from the emotional burden which pressed against his chest like an enormous weight, to clear his mind and heart in a glorious confession, and let whatever happened happen. Yet while he looked upon her as his personal radiant sun, the bright light which illuminated his life and being, he was not blind to the possibilities of a looming darkness in the shape of a gun-toting avenger with fire in his eyes and murder in his heart.

So he held his feelings in check against the crush of emotions which cried out for recognition, realizing that to be alive so as to dream as least gave him a touch of hope. As far as he knew dead men had no dreams, and he certainly was not curious enough to want to find out, sun or no sun. As an antidote against his dread of Stockton he secretly embraced the delicious thought that if Port were killed it would give him a chance with Emily. In his next breath would come pangs of guilt at such uncivil wishes, and in moralistic remorse he would brand them unworthy of him, then cringe like a Sunday pulpit-moralist, avidly praying the gunman couldn't read his mind.

"George," inquired Emily. "Whatever are you pondering over so heavily and deeply? Your brow is so furled-up and such."

He had been replaying Port's confrontation with Engley and Naegelin for the hundredth time, wishing Port had drawn and been erased from existence.

"I was just thinking of all the moving about you seem to have to do on such short notice, how much of a hardship it must be on you."

"You mean every time Port gets into some kind of difficulty?"

"Uh, yes. But mostly all the traveling about. It must be awful unsettling for you."

"Well, it is a disappointment at each move, having to leave newly-made friends and all. And in all that packing and unpacking, too. But I have learned to live light in order not to leave behind the family silver!" she laughed lightly.

"I know what you mean by living light," he agreed. "I been living light fifteen years. But being single, it's never been the task you go through with children and all."

"You ain't married, George?"

"No. Never have,"

""What? A healthy, handsome, strapping brute like you?" she chirped teasingly, looking over her shoulder at him with a cocked head and impish smile that tore at his heart. "Land sakes, you surely are wasting your years."

"Oh, I did think on it some, to be honest, once or twice. But, uh, I don't know."

"Don't know what?"

He found her direct manner enchanting, although highly unexpected. In his mooning he had cast her in the mold of a sedate, semi-helpless and silently suffering creature awaiting someone, him, to steal her away from a life of piller-to-post existence.

"I just," he fumbled, "just never found someone I wanted to spend my life with, I reckon. There are so many unhappy examples out there it makes me extra-cautious."

"Oh, that's for certain. I've seen my share of couples at odds and wretchedly lashed together."

It was his profound hope that she were one of "them" couples who were at odds, that she was awaiting her chance to flee, to escape the confines of an unbearable marriage with a more palatable mate. He looked over at her peripherally in wonder at her beauty. Her green eyes sparkled in the rays of the early rising sun, and her flowing ebony hair undulated loosely in the breeze in velvet waves, occasionally giving off flickering highlights of bronze and auburn. Beneath the angular rays her face glowed a creamy softness. She recalled to him a painting he had seen in an art book years back he never forgot. The woman was standing naked on a giant seashell which floated on an ocean wave, her long tresses unbound and shimmering in the breeze. Rooted in time she gazed toward one side of the viewer as she was being blown toward shore. In his mind she was pensive, distant, almost sad, and he wondered what she was thinking. Was she searching, too? *Emily and the sea waiting for me.* He tore his glance forward with an effort and sat like a block of wood not trusting his emotions, his desire for her, attempting to divorce himself from his secret thoughts which pummeled him constantly. He wanted to continue the conversation, to say something, anything, without putting his foot in his mouth or his neck in a noose.

"Where in Texas do you all come from?" he blurted.

"Cleburne, south of Dallas about twenty miles. Fact is I was born in Texas while my older brothers and sisters were born in Tennessee and Mississippi. Ellen and me are first cousins, and she was born in Texas, too. And where you from?"

"California," he lied.

"Oh, my. I hear that is a pretty country, with the ocean and all. You still have folks there?"

"No. I was orphaned young," he lied again. "Never knew my folks."

"Oh, how sad. Were you adopted at all?"

"When I was about twelve. But it was awful, with the two of them drinking and fighting all the time. So I just run off at fourteen and never went back. My father was a tyrant and a drunk."

"Lord, George. Terrible you don't have a family."

"Oh, ain't so bad," he martyred, playing for sympathy. "I think I done fine for myself, considering." *His mother was a spooked and frayed hostage. Hell with them*

"Oh, my, yes. And I know people speak well of you. I have heard so."

"That's good to hear, thank you."

"And let me tell you, Port thinks right highly of you. He is not a man to take to people easily, but he thinks the world of you, George. He trusts you completely."

At her unwelcome enthusiastic endorsement George suddenly felt drenched in ice water, and an uncontrollable chill fled through him. "I'm, I'm complemented he feels that way."

Momentarily wracked with fear, the thought of flight gripped him. Why did he lie about his background? Although a Louisianan and not from California, he had kin in the area. An aunt for instance in Farmington, and what if Port knew of her? But no, that would be a long shot. Looking at Emily again he was calmed but knew he had to be careful what tales he invented for his benefit, to pull her sympathy toward him. She was his emotional anchor, the end to his internal vacancy, his abstract grail of acceptance. Yet in reaching out to sate his needs he failed to take in the consideration he would be cancelling out another man's dreams, kicking in another man's sand castle, and in this case, potentially terminating his own life. "At least," he stammered, "in all your travels you have seen a lot of the country."

"That is surely true. But this last journey seemed the best, though. And the children had such a good time. It was like a long picnic to them, romping and playing their hearts out. Porter, too, seemed in a better frame of mind, like the change away from Otero was good for him."

George wanted to add that the people in all of Colfax County undoubtedly also rejoiced at his departure. He had already heard by the grapevine about Port's "invitation" to leave Otero.

"I never been to Texas," spoke George. "Is it anything like out here?"

"Not where we were. It was awful desolate with boiling summers. I love it better out here, with the mountains, lakes and rivers. And the cooler temperatures, since it's much higher."

"One thing I recall Ike saying was that there was a lot of cattle raised there for a time, but farming kept pushing the ranchers west."

"Yes, that's true enough. Farmers kept moving in and plowing and fencing until herders were forced to find new pastures. And free grazing is nearing the end, they say. Fact, that's why Irwin Lacy and Lewis Coleman combined their herds and trailed to New Mexico on the Goodnight Trail. Port and Ike worked for them for years."

"Ain't the Stocktons somewhere related to Lacy?"

"Yes, they are. Mrs. Lacy is their first cousin."

"And Lacy now is a partner to George Thompson of Trinidad, after leaving Coleman and New Mexico."

"Yes, he is. And between the two Ike says they own thousands of cattle that roam for miles east and west between Animas City and Trinidad. Ike is happy as Lacy's foreman, hoping to get his own herd soon."

Emily's estimation was not too much of an exaggeration. After severing his partnership with Coleman a few years after their move to Colfax County from Texas, Lacy moved his herds north to Colorado and hooked up with Thompson. He also opened a butcher shop in Fort Lewis, west of Animas City across the La Plata River. His partner in the venture was John Freeland, but unknown to Lacy the shop was surreptitiously used as a slaughterhouse for stolen cattle by the Stockton gang. Woods himself had moved a handful there now and then following a trip south of the Colorado line with a few members of the gang. Ike was not shy about weeding out some of Lacy-Thompson cows either, Lacy not realizing he was mislaying his trust in Ike as his range foreman. Their disappearance, when sometimes "discovered," were of course blamed on them thieving Coe rascals in New Mexico across the line. But when Thompson, who was nobody's fool, unhesitatingly let Lacy know of Ike's disloyalty, Lacy wouldn't believe him, Ike being a kin from his wife's side of the family. Thompson could only shake his head at such blind trust and await his time.

"I understand Port's buddy Clay Allison was also in the employ of Lacy and Coleman," commented Woods.

"Yes, he was their foreman in Texas and responsible for the final drives to New Mexico. That's how Clay got his start in ranching, part of his pay being in cattle after their move to Colfax County."

"Too bad Ike and Port didn't get their draw in cows."

"Well, Port was never much interested in raising cattle for a living, feeling it tied him down too much, although he ain't shy at cow work. But Ike was quite put off, in his own mind thinking he should of got more than just wages. So Lacy did give him a few cows after the last drive."

"Well, with them three as drovers I am certain neither Lacy or Coleman had no worry over rustlers."

"I should say not. Them three was the best insurance they could have had."

"Ike still looks forward to owning his own ranch and herd. He seems really ambitious in that direction from what he always says."

"Yes, and I hope it's real soon in his future. Poor Ellen is not too keen on moving about as me, and would like to see a settled-down life. She would be happy to see it all happen."

George had never seen or met Ellen but heard she was even more attractive than Emily. Yet to hear the way Ike talked it was not a marriage made in heaven, and he was not bashful in finding his choice of female companionship in one of the local whorehouses, especially now in rambunctiously randy Durango, new and still bursting at the seams with new people every day. Woods also found Ike's company easier to be in, although he too had the soul of a timber rattler, and not hesitant to kill if the situation arose. He was just smarter to keep his murderous side under wraps, and played more at being more surface-sociable, and smoother to get along with.

"Do Ike and Port figure to settle down hereabouts permanently, or do they plan on returning to Texas one day?"

"Oh, no, out here is where they aim to stay. Or at least Ike will, especially after he sets up his ranch. Port of course may move on as usual, but never back to Texas. He had such a falling out with their father that nothing will ever drag him back there."

"And how was that?"

"The long and short of it all was that Porter was in such a fit of temper during an argument with his pappy he whipped him on the front porch with his rifle butt. He would have kilt him too, if Ike hadn't pulled him off. Both brothers left right after on a cattle drive to Kansas."

Woods raised his eyebrows over that piece of news, wondering what more surprises was in store for him concerning Port. "Yessiree," he whistled. "Ol' Port is a man of few words when it comes to settling a difference of opinion, isn't he?"

"Oh, my lord, George! There runs my mouth! I should *not* have mentioned such a thing! I know Porter would not approve, so please, *please,* don't breath a word of what I said! Not to anyone, promise?"

"You have my word, Emily. I surely won't"

"Oh, thank you, George," she breathed gratefully, gripping his forearm a moment in gratitude. "Sometimes I rattle on so, not thinking. But it is so natural a feeling, talking to you. You feel like an old friend and all, you know?"

"And I feel the same with you, Emily. And you can trust me, for I don't betray confidences.

Most certainly never in your case. So you can rest easy."

It gave him the feeling of having the edge to have her in his trust, a secret imparted from her for his safe keeping. And her hand squeezing his arm for that brief second sent a thrill shooting through him which left him emotionally reeling. It took all his strength and will power not to slip his arm around her shoulders and pull her to him, to tell her how safe she was with him, forever.

The Las Animas River flowed alongside them to their right, and on the far bank a half-dozen deer stood watching their passing cautiously, while several bent to quench themselves from the river. A red fox on their side scurried away followed by a pair of pups, then suddenly next to their wagon a covey of quail whistled in clustered flight. He continued stealing glances toward her peripherally, so as not to make it obvious. At times he would slouch back as if to change position so he could stare at her rocking, swaying back, enjoying the supple movements of her torso and wavy hair flowing in the breeze. Now and then they would ride the saddle horses to break the monotony, he taking the reins of the wagon as the children pretended they were in charge of the team. In his reverie he would imagine they were his family he was leading along the countryside, his wife and daughters, back to their home, their domicile. Then he would catch himself on the brink of speaking of his feelings and quickly bite his tongue mentally.

It was close to a fifty mile drive from Durango to Ike's, much of it paralleling the river. Earlier, Emily had contemplated visiting the O'Neals near the state line at Ignacio, old friends of Erath County days, perhaps even staying overnight. But she changed her mind, anxious to be with Port. She was also excited over seeing Ellen again, whom she had not laid eyes on in almost five years, since Ike had left Cimarron for Lincoln. It would be a real holiday for both.

"You say Ellen was not too happy over her having to move about?" asked George.

"Not hardly. She's more a town person and wishes for a permanent home life. Traipsing about the land eats away at her domestic wishes more and more each year. I'm the other way, and don't care for cities hardly at all. I'm getting like Porter in that I can hardly stay put for long."

"Something good to be said for both, but I can sure get fed up with town-crowds awful quick. Animas City is city enough for me, and Durango's a zoo already."

On they drove until at late sunset they pulled into a small grove of trees and brush off the road for the night. About half-way point, they were a few miles south of the Colorado border. A supper of canned sardines, peaches and bread layered with butter suited them enough, being more road-weary than hungry. In a short time the females bundled themselves up in blankets in the wagon bed and dropped off to sleep in moments. George stayed awake for a time, listening guardedly, walking about now and then. He mounted his horse several times and slowly wandered about in wide circles. Not really worried about their safety he still liked to be cautious on the road, especially in open, desolate country miles from nowhere. Perhaps it was habit developed from his occasional rustling activities, where one had to be cautious and aware of his immediate environment, or else. Too, they were near Coe country, and he didn't relish running across any of the enemy alone with no back-up. After nearly two hours he began feeling more at ease, so decided to turn in. He found a brushy, near-concealed abutment near the wagon just in case. Still, he dozed but fitfully.

The early dawn awoke him before the others and he stirred quietly unmoving, looking about from his concealment. Satisfied, he stood and peered toward the wagon and could see the bundled bodies and smiled, knowing they had slept better than he did. It elated him to feel their protector, warmed him immensely. Stretching his creaking joints he yawned and checked out the staked mules and horses, gave them some feed, walked them to water, then went to the wagon to wake Emily. Together they prepared a double-hearty breakfast to make up for the light supper; scrambled eggs, steak, beans, biscuits spread with jam or butter, all topped off with hot coffee.

Unwittingly, on George and Emily's drive through mushrooming Durango early the previous morning, they were witness to the future death knell of Animas City. The frontier hamlet, said to have boasted of a population of 3,000 at its peak, would soon undergo the transmogrification of being devoured by the bursting new railroad settlement of Durango.

Animas City had begun its life in the early 1870s as a trading and supply post to the scattered silver and gold camps in the rugged La Plata mountains. Gradually, farmers and ranchers were drawn to the new land, settling up and down the lush and fertile Animas River valley. The village on the river soon boasted a school, bank, law office, lumber mill, livery stable, butcher shop, three drug stores, two blacksmiths, several doctors, three saloons and a church. Wishing a sense of permanence, a town-site was surveyed in 1876, and in 1878 incorporated. A flour mill and sawmill made their appearance in 1879 along with coal mining. By 1880 the village grew to 500.

Generally quiet and rustic, only a few times was its pastoral serenity seriously threatened. One night in 1877 a drunken cowboy named Pitt West galloped up and down Main Street in a howling rage shooting off his revolver. He had earlier slain a man in an altercation and now was "hurrahing" the village. He was so terrifying and out of control that Mayor Engley and sheriff Bob Dwyer fled in fear to the nearby military cantonment for safety. Meanwhile the aggravated citizenry stirred enough in a demonstration of swift justice to swat him efficiently. Jerked off his horse, West was enthusiastically pummeled for a time, then taken to the nearest tree and left to hang.

It was during the winter of 1879-1880 that the beginning of the end of its brief pastoral existence arrived. It came in the form of the Denver & Rio Grande Railroad laying track westward.

Arriving just south of Animas City, the route of the tracks took a turn north aiming for the town of Silverton, fifty miles north. The railroad would be a boon to the gold and silver camps throughout the vicinity, and the company had earlier presented its plans before Animas City, offering to make it the railroad center. But the honor was refused, for the concessions demanded by the D & RG were felt too stringent. Unruffled, the railroaders set up their scruffy tent-town two miles south of town, calling the primitive settlement Durango, and Silverton the following year became an end-of-track town.

Through the spring and summer of 1880 hammers thumped and saws cut and shovels dug from dawn til dusk, covering the landscape with a wide collection of man-made fabrications. Over the months the wild and rough gandy dancers were joined by a wilder and rougher collection of gunmen, gamblers, thieves, whores and hustlers of every stripe and ambition. Businessmen and merchants too, honest and dishonest, enlisted their presence, stimulated by the aroma of freshly slain roadkill. For years, expansion and progress, the ambiguous offsprings of Manifest Destiny, continued sprawling westward in all its glory, dragging populations behind it by the scruff of their necks, creating a multitude of hamlets, burgs, towns and cities to flaunt each day their arm-pitted presence. Civilization was on the move and waited for no one, and neither did Durango.

It was on the morning of 13 September that George and Emily and her three children rode south from Animas City through the noisily bustling village, bursting restlessly from its tent-town status, on their way to Ike's in New Mexico. The wide dirt street was littered and jammed with horses, mules, wagons and early rising citizens scurrying about like an army of preoccupied ants on a mission.

"Good Lord, George," exclaimed Emily in amazement. "I ain't seen this much goings-on since years ago in Dallas! Ain't it crazy?"

Later that afternoon a surveyor's stake was pounded into the earth to officially give birth to the newly born town of Durango, demonstrating irrefutably the impending demise of two-year-old Animas City, which would slip slowly into obscurity like a departed uncle.

By November Durango bloomed with seven hotels and restaurants, eleven saloons, two bakeries, two blacksmiths, and a variety of dance halls, meat markets and general stores. They were bolstered by a population of 2,000, with more arrivals each day. Soon, Animas City merchants and residents commenced a gradual exodus into the promising arms of Durango as bees to honey, abandoning their former nest like faithless lovers. With the nibbling process of mastication the minuscule community's unavoidable end was in sight, to the chagrin of those who remained.

Over the ensuing years it was reality which finally sank the tiny burg; her need for water and its massive debt to her big city kin. Surrendering to the inevitable, Animas City would officially be welcomed into the arms of Durango on 1 January 1948, after an annexation vote the previous year of 294 for and 114 against.

FOUR

Like birthing Durango, Ike's fledgling flock of followers had been in existence but several months. They previously had been known as the Eskridge gang, a collection of local riffraff led by a pair of brothers from New Jersey, Harg and Dyson. Little more than uncivil rowdies, they mostly busied themselves with hoisting beer and rooster-strutting about tiny Animas City, practicing petty thievery and making off with an occasioned purloined cow or sheep. Nothing dangerous enough to lead the more solid citizens to bring out the hemp, only enough to have a few comment or grumble on their bad manners and ill behavior. But Stockton envisioned something more opportunistic on the horizon, having a natural corporate turn of mind, and since he possessed the necessary qualities of a leader, he convinced the gang he was their man on horseback. After Ike took over rulership of the group they were referred to as the Stockton-Eskridge Gang, with Harg his lieutenant.

With careful planning and low-key maneuvering Stockton slowly created a firm power base.

In keeping a tight rein on his men and their antics within the city limits, he was insured their tolerance by the townspeople. He was also smart enough to make certain they concentrated their rustling south of the Colorado boundary and to take only New Mexico cattle, since the extensive open range was grazed by herders on both sides of the line. They were soon at war with a faction of rustlers in New Mexico led by George and Frank Coe, a pair of cousins lately of the Lincoln County War who fled north to Farmington out of survival. The incongruity of it was that Stockton's followers for a time were looked upon by the Coloradans as a bunch of "good ol' boys" fighting off the outlaws of New Mexico, disparagingly referred to as the "Lincoln County Mob."

Even the editor of the Rico *Dolores News* glowingly championed them. The irony of it, the Coes and Stocktons, although now deadly enemies, had once been warm friends years previous in Colfax County. And the darker tale yet, was that most of the arriving cattlemen of Farmington eventually formed a cold-blooded bloc and forced many of the farmers out of the area. Originally called "a farming town," the settlers agreed upon the name of Farmington in 1879 after laying out the townsite.

Four years previously, after Ike broke Port out of jail in Cimarron, he smartly bade goodbye to the area and headed south, ending up in Lincoln, New Mexico running a bar. George and Frank Coe, farmers back then, also vacated Colfax County following instructions from Sheriff Pete Burleson and deputy Mace Bowman to leave local stock alone or else. In a short time the Coes emerged in Lincoln town and reacquainted themselves with Ike. In the conflict that broke out in the late 1870s, known as the Lincoln County War, the Coes and Ike favored the Chisum-McSween-Tunstall coalition, the side Billy the Kid fought on. While the Coes were a bit more active, Ike remained behind his bar, using the place as an information-gathering center for their faction.

When the war came to its bloody climax in July 1878 after the five-day siege and battle at the John Henry Tunstall house, and with the killing of Tunstall, many of the participants scattered. The Coes, having had their ranch stripped and burned to the ground later that year by a band of renegades led by the notorious John Selman, returned to Colfax County to help move kith, kin and kine westward to Farmington. Ike likewise in time exited Lincoln, showing up in Farmington with his wife and daughter. They lived in with the Coes for a spell until moving to a ranch farther east.

In the spring of 1880, George Coe's cousin Lou had to go to court in Farmington in answer to a suit brought against him by a farmer who claimed Lou's cattle trampled and ruined his crops. Also present with George that day was Ike Stockton, who suggested they attend. Both men were of course armed, being the accepted uniform-of-the-day. Before proceedings commenced in the courtroom, Judge Halford ordered that all the spectators be disarmed. Refusing to do so, Ike and George rose and left the room to linger in the yard. The court deputies were Harge and Dison Eskeridge, and the brothers firmly informed the two men that they must disarm or leave the premises. It was not a chore both men found tasteful, and Ike carried it farther with a heated argument. George Coe, rather than relinquish his revolver, decided he would return home. Ike continued his cursing contest with Harge Eskridge until he thought it time to put a stop to all the talk and drew his Colt. Unknown to him his worn cylinder pin had come loose with the embarrassing result of the cylinder dropping to the ground at his feet, bullets and all. Now holding little more than the frame of his revolver in his fist, cocked but useless, he threw it aside and made for his saddle gun. As he was about to withdraw his Winchester and go into action, Coe, on horseback and about to leave, sensibly saw where everything was heading and wisely decided to put a stop to it. He quickly drew his Colt and aimed it at Stockton and ordered him not to draw his rifle.

"Let's get on outta here, Ike. To hell with court. We didn't come here for trouble."

"God damn it, George, I ain't taking no shit from that piss-ant tin-horn badge carrier!"

"I said *leave* it!" emphasized Coe as he cocked his hammer. "Pick up your gun and cylinder and let's get! Now!"

Grudgingly plucking his fallen cylinder, bullets and gun from the dirt, Ike climbed into the saddle and the two rode out. A short while later Ike and his wife and daughter moved from Farmington, but that day Ike rode fuming in silence, not taking Coe's pointed six-gun in sensible stride. He felt it demeaned him in the eyes of all present. The shaming insult to his manhood etched itself into his heart, and he vowed to kill Coe the first chance he got to save face.

After Ike moved his family to Animas City he shrewdly set about making amends to the Eskridge brothers and lay out his plans of hitting the New Mexico herds. He combined his thirst for vengeance with his scheme of rustling, encouraged by the economic opportunities presented by the booming railroad town of Durango. Also to his joy Animas City was in the market for a lawman, and after laying the groundwork wrote to Port in Otero.

Port was more than ready to leave, finally having over-stayed his welcome by a handful of bullet-ridden bodies. Several months prior Port had shot William Withers in Otero, claiming it was a case of mistaken identity. He thought it was a local deputy, "Hurricane" Bill Martin, whom he held a grudge against for once having had the nerve to attempt arresting him. Too, a pair of previous murders continued to plague him after a grand jury issued a true bill for them four years earlier. But no one was motivated enough to bring the cold-blooded killer to bay, and as a result he was free to continue his talent for keeping the local population nervous. He was finally apprehended in Trinidad, Colorado, twenty miles north of Raton. The law captured and jailed him on a fugitive warrant for the murder of Antonio Arcibia. Colfax County Sheriff Isaiah Rinehart gladly made the journey to bring him down to lock him up in Cimarron's jail, but a day later brother Ike shoved a gun in the jailer's side, and Port was free again. Ike immediately and smartly dispatched himself and his family several counties south to Lincoln, realizing the law wouldn't take kindly to playing his brother's rescuer. Port took his wife and two kids southerly also, but only to Glorieta, a small village east of Santa Fe. Yet Port's short temper never allowed him long-distance planning, and before too long he shot and wounded a man over a difference of opinion. On the trail again, he returned unfazed and prodigal-like to his Otero-Cimarron haunts.

One afternoon he received a letter from Ike. Being illiterate he took it to a part-time school teacher to decipher. In it was a check and a short note summoning him to Animas City. Only too happy to be on the road again he raced home to tell Emily to gather what she could for another journey. That night he rode into Cimarron to borrow a wagon and a pair of mules for the trip. As he rode homeward leading the mules and wagon by a tether, he stopped to quench his thirst at a local cantina on the edge of town. A half-dozen bottles of beer later, as he emerged into the night and started to climb into the saddle, he was accosted by a pair of grim-faced men with drawn six-shooters, cocked and ready. They were lawmen Sheriff Pete Burleson and deputy Mace Bowman. Port stood immobile with his left hand still gripping the saddle horn and left foot frozen in the stirrup, breezily asking, "Well, howdy, Mace, Pete. What's up?" Furtively, Port's right paw slid over his holster, thumbing off its hammer-thong.

"Stand exactly like you are, Port," instructed Bowman quietly as he nudged the gunman's side with his Colt. "Don't move an inch." Burleson stepped before him to set his weapon against Port's mid-section. "We are going to make this short and sweet," continued Bowman. "You just listen and pay extra close attention. I'll only say this once. We are an un-welcoming committee to see that you leave town. Pronto. You will leave Otero town and Colfax County behind like it is a bad memory and never return. Understand?"

"Yes sir, I-I do. I will. Fact is, I am in the process of leaving in the morning."

"No," corrected Bowman. "Tonight." He then placed the barrel of his revolver against Port's nose, cocking it slowly three, four, five times. Stockton in helpless anxiety eyed the bullets in the cylinder as they rotated with metallic clicks inches from his face.

Bowman continued. "We are sick of your senseless killings and your laughing in everyone's face over them. You are history here. You dare come back and you are a dead man. Comprende?"

Face glistening with perspiration Port did not dare nod, so gasped, "O.k., Mace, Pete, sure, of course. You all will never see me again, hear?"

"We hear," acknowledged Burleson. "We heard good. For your sake we hope you do."

Bowman lowered his weapon but kept it at waist level, still pointed and cocked. He reached over nonchalantly and rehooked Stockton's hammer thong. "Climb aboard. Port. And have a safe journey."

Without looking back Stockton rode in a hasty trot to leave his now stale hunting grounds forever, glad to be alive, the tethered mule and wagon trundling along behind him.

FIVE

As George and the Stockton females were finishing up their breakfast, a bit of action was bestirring itself twenty-some miles east of Ike's ranch at Lew Coe's place near Farmington. Agitated and horseback, Hiram Cox, the Constable of Farmington, was in conversation with Lew who was standing on his front porch. Astride his mount, the lawman inquired if he had been missing any stock lately.

"You, know, I am missing a few head again. I thought they was maybe wandering around in the hills, but I couldn't find a one."

"Well," sighed Cox. "I got to admit missing four or five cows the other day. Seems like someone's still picking a few here and there from different herds. Others been complaining, too."

"It's that damn Stockton bunch, I bet."

"Won't disagree there."

"Cousin George and me have an idea which way they might be taking them."

"Far from here?"

"Maye eight, ten miles. From there we think they relay them north, into Colorado."

"Hmmm. Why don't we ride on out there now? Got time?"

"You bet. And let's take George. He's hot to handle them culprits."

The constable and his freshly deputized duo galloped north in the brisk morning with rifles, six-guns and a look of business in their eyes. They rode north along the east bank of the shallow La Plata River, crossing over below the village of La Plata. The Coes suspected the rustlers probably had an encampment a bit west and north of the tiny settlement, sort of a temporary rallying point for the stolen stock.

From there, they theorized, they were then driven five miles to the New Mexico-Colorado state line where others took over, running them farther north where they were sold or butchered.

The country was wide and broad, swept with long rolling hills, and chopped up with enough dry arroyos and shallow canyons to break the monotony. The bright sun in the clear blue sky took most of the chill out of the air. Patches of old snow, much of it greyed, lay in many isolated islands, and in the distance the snowy peaks of the San Juans in Colorado stood in bold relief.

After close to a ten-mile lope, and northwest of La Plata, the men spotted a thin wisp of smoke. They automatically fanned out and unsheathed their Winchesters, quietly cranking a round in the chamber. Secluded in a low draw with his back to them, a lone cowboy squatted before the small fire intently gnawing on a piece of roasted beef. The three rode slowly forward until about thirty feet away and stopped, rifles leveled.

"Hands up and don't move!" ordered the constable. "And be damn quick about it!"

The man wisely froze, trying to peer over his shoulder.

"That's right," added Lew. "Don't make a move. Now stand slow and easy, and keep reaching."

Obediently he raised both arms high, a piece of chewed meat in his right hand. Within moments he was relieved of his revolver. He turned cautiously. Tall, gaunt and grimy with a four—or five day beard, and grubby-clothed to boot, he appeared quite trail worn.

"Didn't mean to interrupt your feast," apologized Cox, "but who are you?"

"My name is Bill Anderson, strangers," he answered with a confident air behind a rock-hard smile, eyeing his rifle resting against a boulder only inches away.

Lew, knowing his intent, and who already had the man's six gun shoved behind his own gun belt, purposely walked over and claimed it.

"Easy with that rifle, runt," bristled the man sarcastically as he began to lower his hands, momentarily forgetting he was unarmed.

"Runt?" asked Lew, casually aiming it at the stranger's forehead as he cocked the hammer.

Arms stretching higher yet, meat-covered bone still in one hand, the man looked back and forth at George and Hiram who stood sphinx-like on either side of him. He felt as of he had just stepped into a bottomless pit and was sinking deeper.

"Well, I mean, I mean," he faltered. "No offence, y'know?"

"No offence?" smiled Lew. "Well, thank you. I feel a comfort already."

Cox asked off-handedly, "Bill Anderson you say your name is?"

"Yes, sir," he replied evenly, eyeing Cox's badge.

"People call you 'Tex' by any chance?"

"Yes, sir," he roostered proudly. "Cause that's where I'm from."

"Well, now. I'm the constable from Farmington and it seems I got some news on you."

"Oh?" he spoke with discomfort.

"Seems you shot a man up in Silverton, Colorado a while ago, Mister William 'Tex' Anderson."

"Uh, that's so, now that I recollect, mister constable. Self-defense, though, strictly self-defense."

"Before that you went by the alias 'Charley Smith' at Fort Griffin, Texas. That's where you had to leave hasty-like for stealing a horse."

"Naw, naw," Tex shook his head. "That can be cleared up."

"You then went to Chalk Creek, Colorado where you killed a man."

"Naw, naw, that too was self-defense."

"That's a fine pair of oxen you got there, Tex," complimented Cox.

""Uh, well," he struggled. "Funny thing about them, constable. As I was eating my meal awhile ago, here, them two showed up. Don't know who they belong to or where they come from."

"Hear that, boys?" Cox nodded his head. "Ain't that a funny coincidence?"

"Yeah," smiled George toward Lew. "Makes me want to giggle."

"Truely is amusing," grinned Lew.

"By the looks of them brands on them oxen, cowboy," Cox continued. "I would say they belong to Pete Fox. Know him quite well."

"Really now?" remarked Tex. "Well, he'll be awful pleased to have them back, I'm sure."

"Yes, he will," answered the constable. "In fact I got word this morning someone stole them last night."

"Well, I ain't the one took them." protested Tex indignantly. "The thief must of got scared off!"

"I'm sure he did. And by the way, how's that beef? Tasty enough for you?"

"Well, uh, now that you mention it, just fine."

"How'd you come by that carcass, anyways?"

"Well, another funny thing, y'know? A couple herders shared camp with me last night. They had this young cow with them they killed this morning for breakfast and shared it with me. After eating, they left."

"Well, Tex, I'm complimented you found that beef tasty, 'cause the brand reads as one of mine."

"Oh, Gawd! You mean they done took one of your cows? That's terrible! And I bet them fellows thieved them oxen!"

Cox shook his head in lamentation saying, "Such brazen lies from the mouth of one man in such short order I ain't heard in all my days. Your slathering and slobbering tales is downright embarrassing, Tex. Fact is, you should be wearing a bib to protect your shirt."

Shame-faced, Tex stared down at his feet as if he might find solace there.

"Let me tell you what happened. You and your friends moseyed on through last day or two picking up a cow or two from different herds here and there. Along the way you passed Pete Fox's place and couldn't resist them lovely oxen. Your friends spent the night here, then left you as watch-out on their back trail while they ran the stolen creatures on into Colorado. We're taking you in. Let's go."

Tex saw it was useless to protest or lie any further, so complied in quiet resignation. With the mounted prisoner's wrists tied behind his back, Cox led the man's horse by the reins. The Coes followed on flank, each leading an ox. After about a mile the procession stopped along the bank of the La Plata under several cottonwoods, one of which thrust a beckoning arm. The constable's eye caught an envelope working its way out of Tex's rear pocket, so reached and plucked it out.

"What we have here, young fellow? A bill of sale? Your will, maybe?"

"Uh, a letter from my wife."

The constable read aloud. "'My dear Bill. I have received two letters from you, but ma told me today that I should never write to you, but I can write this without her knowing it. Oh, my darling, I thought we would have such pleasant times this summer, and you are gone. I can never be happy again. Oh, I have never, never suffered so in my mind in my life, as I have since you killed that man. To think the only man I ever loved has the stains of a man's blood on his soul. It nearly killed me to see you so sour the morning you left. I may never see you again in this world. Everyone around here says it is nothing for you to kill a man. It hurts me awfully to hear them talk so about my darling. You never gave me room to doubt your word; you was always true to me in everything and in every way. But, Bill, you know you done wrong to go in that saloon. I have no doubt that the man you killed meant to rob you. But still, I can hardly give you up, it does not seem like home without you. I cannot enjoy myself without you.

"'I went up to your cabin the other day and saw your violin hanging on the wall, and I wondered if I will ever hear you play again?

"'I measured myself yesterday; I am five feet four and weigh 122 pounds. The baby doesn't show yet. If I never see you again I will always think the same of you. All alone you have gone and left me, and no other's bride I'll I be, for tomorrow I will be gone. Forgive me. Your wife, Allie Anderson.'"

The constable, pale and visibly shaken, crushed the pages and threw them into the Texan's face. "God damn you to hell!" he seethed. "You even murder at a distance! Well, now it's your turn, widower."

"P-p-please," trembled Anderson. Let me explain . . . ."

"She already done all the explaining you need!" Cox cut him off. Turning to the Coes he continued. "Boys, we are now surrounded by fifteen desperate masked men who have disarmed us and taken our captive. We can only protest to the injustice of it, as we helplessly sit and watch it all, knowing their cruel intent."

"That's right," agreed Lew.

"Yep, nasty shame," echoed George.

"Don't constable, please," implored Tex. "Just let me go and I'll never come back. I promise to leave the country, honest!"

"What?" snarled Cox. "And have you be a burden and a pestilence to some ranchers down the road?"

"But I didn't kill your cow, honest! I was just eating what they cooked up! And I was about to return them oxen this morning, knowing they done wrong!"

In silent disgust, the lawman leaned over and took the prisoner's coiled rope from his saddle. Tossing an end of it across a tree limb and grabbing it as it fell, he wound the it around Tex's neck, fashioning a hasty noose.

"Please don't, constable," wailed Anderson, now shaken at his fate. *"Please!!"*

He was ignored completely as Cox leaned toward the tree and fastened the rope to a broken nub of a branch. He then walked his horse to the rear of Tex's and gave his mount a swift kick, yelling, "Giddy-up, dammit, giddy-up!"

Tex's bay shot forward, cutting his shrill cries short as he was left swinging and swirling and kicking air.

"There sways the son of a bitch who ate my beef without my invite," announced the constable. "And if there's one thing I won't tolerate, it's a rude guest. You boys go on home. I'll deliver these oxen to Fox." He then turned and led the lumbering animals away. With him he took Anderson's Winchester, needing one to replace his occasionally malfunctioning piece.

As the Coes rode toward Farmington they took a final look at their suspended work. The fugitive's bladder and bowels had burst and surrendered its contents, and what was left of his life trickled and seeped steamily onto the ground.

"That's one hellova price to pay for a stolen meal," spoke George.

"Well," grinned Lew. "Nothing I like better than civilizing the uncouth."

They turned and loped back toward their ranch. Lew led the rustler's horse and trappings, while George had the man's six gun and belted ammunition looped across his saddle horn.

SIX

Hardly a week later the Animas City *Southwest* lambasted the lynching as an "atrocious murder." Normally, low-life varmints such as horse thieves, cow-thieves and killers—and Anderson marvelously fit all three categories—were usually dispatched with the same degree of regret one would have for a poisonous scorpion or noxious weed. But the Coes' thirst for justice backfired, because Ike Stockton, never one to pass up an opportunity, much less give a friend or foe an even break, used Tex's necktie party as a chance to get in his digs at his former cohorts. Ike was actually happy it was the Texan they had strung up, for this late member of his confederation he quickly grew to distrust and despise, whose not-too-bright bragging and swaggering he was convinced was no asset to his group. So the Coes had not only done his dirty work for him, they unwittingly assisted in making Tex Anderson a martyr for Stockton's purposes.

Shortly after Ike was appraised of Tex's suspension, he purposely sought out the publisher and editor of the *Dolores News* in Rico, Charles Adams Jones, whom he met once.

"Good afternoon, Mister Jones."

"Why, hello, Mister Stockton."

"Have you heard the latest atrocity that them damned Coes have committed south of our fair, law-loving border?"

"Well, uh, no, sir. I don't believe so."

"Then allow me to relate it to you in all its goriness and insult to liberty, my good man. Those bunch of cut-throats are running about like a pack of foamy-mouthed coyotes. Nobody is safe any more. The other day they took an innocent cowboy, new to the area from Texas and whom I knew slightly, and unkindly lynched him. It appears it was for no better reason than he was grazing his tiny herd across the line in New Mexico. It is a sad thing too, for he left behind him in Texas a broken-hearted and freshly married pregnant wife. Bill Anderson was his name. "Tex" to his friends, of whom I was proudly one."

"Why, good lord! This is abominable, Mister Stockton!"

"Yes, it is," agreed Stockton indignantly as he continued for the better part of an hour, feeding the editor's fired-up head with lurid details of mis- and disinformation.

The resulting story and the newspaper's condemnation of the crass deed was the opening wedge between the two area's cattle raisers. The *News* played the item for all it was worth, adding bitingly that it appeared Colorado stockmen were not welcome to graze their cattle on New Mexico grass, regardless of the rule of open free range. The paper additionally labeled the Coes, "the Lincoln County Mob." Following this, the Durango *Record* chimed in, calling the New Mexico faction the "Coe Consolidation."

From Farmington, Frank Coe hastily wrote to the Rico *News* protesting the charges and to explain the particulars, but to no avail. Ike had beat him to it with a good scoop the paper couldn't resist, and they fed upon it as a tasty steak. It's co-publisher, Frank Hartman, let Coe know editorially that they were nothing but "rope-pulling cowards." He added that he had received numerous letters from New Mexico describing the deteriorating situation "down there," and condemned Coe for embracing vigilante law over legal jurisprudence. In this case it was the old story of chickens coming home to roost, for Hartman was earlier run out of Farmington for his outspoken editorials there. He was the very last man Coe should have aired his problems to. Also, Ike, to his good fortune, had several mining claims in Rico where he and several of his compadres spent time, so made sure he continuously endeared himself to Hartman's boss, editor Jones.

"Yessiree, Charlie," eulogized Stockton again and again each time they "happened" to meet on the street. "The power of the press is the people's weapon for justice, and I think it is wonderful of you to let them Lincoln County lawbreakers know it! Keep up the good work, Charlie! Me and my boys will back you up all the way."

"That I shall, Ike, that I shall! And I want you to know our paper too is behind you one-hundred percent. It excites me to the bones to know we have the likes of you and your men on our side in this fight for justice, prepared to mount the barricades against those lawless hoodlums on our behalf."

"You got that right, Charlie. You can count on us completely!"

Although Ike was a confrontational man, over the years he learned to wisely clothe his temper with diplomacy and tact. As a result, his thinking took on the tenor of a plotter and conniver, with the added outcome of realizing the value of social imaging. He loved the persona he displayed to the unaware of being a concerned citizen, while his men knew he was not a man to be crossed or toyed with. A killer he was, and as deadly as his older brother. But while Port was of such undisguised pugilistic temperament many were nervous merely being in his company, Ike with his calculated social graces appeared the saner of the two. Ike never heard of Machiavelli, but he emulated his dark philosophical principals admirably. Stockton, following a "discussion" with a reporter or editor of one of the regional publications, would often later have a handful of the gang laughing until tears streamed down their faces at how he had Hartman and Jones swallowing anything he said.

"Editor Jones is our personal public relations man, boys," he explained joyfully to the guffawing men. "And it tickles me deliriously to know that we have most of the people around here eating out of our hands."

It wasn't too long before George Coe's Farmington neighbor claimed his cows trashed his crops and demanded restitution. It appears several larcenous farmers schemed to make a few dollars from him by enticing some of Coe's cows to run through their gardens. They then swore out a warrant and took him to court for damages. Although New Mexico did have an ordinance making cattlemen responsible for any damage their cows may incur, it irked Coe that some farmers were creating a small industry of illegally collecting fines with their bogus charges.

"Hell," snarled George. "You ain't got no crops to speak of, and I ain't paying you a dime!"

"We'll see about that!" shouted the farmer as he promptly trod off to the courthouse to commence legal proceedings. The next day an officer appeared on George's doorstep with a warrant.

"What in hell you got there?" queried Coe in short temper, already suspecting what it was.

"A warrant, George, signed by J. P. Halford. I gotta serve you so you can come on down to the courthouse and answer the farmer's charges. Hell, you know the routine."

"You take that warrant and the routine and shove it where the sun don't shine. Now get the hell off my porch!"

"Damn it, George, I'm only doing my job!" answered the deputy to the door slamming in his face. In frustrated anger the lawman walked over to Coe's corral and collected a mule to hold as collateral for the charges. Immediately, a pair of George's friends reclaimed the mule at gun point and drove the deputy off. In a brief time those two were arrested and taken to jail. In a faster piece of time a group led by George and Frank Coe marched down to the cooler and freed their friends, plus drove the presiding Justice of the Peace Halford out of the county. The area became a war zone, with the herders expelling the farmers and their sympathizers out of the region in a power take-over. It was another range war all over again, as illegal force reigned and justice was reined in, allowing mindless six-gun diplomacy ride to the hilt. Unwittingly for a time the local print media of Durango and its environs blindly waved the banner of righteousness on the side of their "team," the Stockton crusaders. Also unfortunately for the Coe contingent, evicted publisher Frank Hartman had accompanied the first forty-some expelled citizens to Colorado. As an editor now for the Rico, *News*, he had the delicious chance for retaliation and he took to it heart and soul. It all played conveniently and unfortunately into Ike's hands, and being a master manipulator, he took the natural next step by donning the mantel of protector of Colorado's turf, and defender of its citizens.

"Look at this," hailed Ike to George Woods, holding a late issue of the Rico *News* before him. The headline shouted in bold print, *"BLACKER THAN HELL!,"* and described the forced exodus of citizens from Farmington, plus the atmosphere of murderous fear which gripped the entire region.

"Unbelievable, Ike," awed George. "But I don't know if I can live up to the virtuous image editor Jones has painted of us."

"Nonsense, George, it's simple. Just tip your hat to the ladies, don't spit on the sidewalk, and keep saying 'maam' or 'sir' to your elders. God will sort out the rest."

SEVEN

One November afternoon Woods was on a sweep through northern New Mexico with a few of the gang. It was a sunny, cloudless day, bright yet bracing, as the six riders wearily pushed two dozen cattle north along the bank of the La Plata toward the Colorado border. It was one of those days when tempers were taut, a bad hair day with not a barber in sight. For some unexplained reason all wished they were elsewhere. Astrologers would probably discern that Uranus was squared with Mars, while Pisces was going to pieces. Port was in charge of the group which included Dison and Harge Eskridge, Jim Garrett and Milt Buchanan. Buchanan had been unrelentingly unloading his distemper over the past hour, and as they approached the state line his bitching grew louder. He and Garrett had been elected by Port to remain overnight at the line while the purloined cows were run up to the Fort Lewis butcher shop. Buchanan wished to be replaced by another for he itched in the worse way to quickly head back to Animas City, hardly 15 miles east of Fort Lewis, into the arms of his waiting amoretta, Rosemarie Smith. But alas, he heard no sympathetic strains from any of the men as to his plight, mainly for being so odiously disliked. Not many could stand Milt Buchanan because of his rancid personality, and as a companion on the trail he could be overly trying on one's patience. The men often wondered why the Stocktons kept him on as a member of their tribe, and they wondered especially why Port hadn't ended his life by this time. They came to the conclusion that Buchanan was Port's appointed court clown, someone he could verbally assault for his personal pleasure and amusement. And while they did sometimes feel sorry for him whenever Stockton toyed with his fate, they were also glad it was not them at the knife-point of Port's prodding.

"Good afternoon, fat boy," greeted Port as he pulled his horse next to his. "I heard someone say you're displeased about camping at the border overnight."

"Aw, naw, P-P-Port," stammered Buchanan. "I was only hoping someone would take my place down here so's I could get back to Animas City sooner."

"Got some important business that can't wait?"

"Yes, yes, that's it!"

"Whyn't you let me know afore we set out on this excursion?"

"I-I-I just forgot in the rush of things, I reckon."

"What was so important that you forgot to mention?"

Buchanan squirmed as the Eskridges snickered, the brothers knowing that Port was having his normal sadistic sport with the mouthy but now nervous cowhand. Garrett and Woods, riding trail, could tell what was taking place ahead of them and looked at each other rolling their eyes and shaking their heads.

"Well," continued Stockton tightly. "Speak up. What was your business that you disremembered and now convenient recall? C'mon, you fat toad. Tell me about it."

Buchanan now knew he was in for it, and up to his nose, and wished he hadn't jabbered so much of his dislike for guard duty. He knew Port wouldn't let go now, but rag him viciously to his satisfaction like a dog chewing a bone. Sweat ran in rivulets down his flaccid face. He didn't know why Port had to constantly pick him out for needling, make him look a fool in front of all the men. He wanted to get down from his horse in the worst way and run and hide someplace. He was so frozen with fear he could not think.

"It's Rosemarie," he blurted suddenly. "I, uh, think she's pregnant."

"*What?* You're lying."

"No, no, honest! I wouldn't lie about a thing like that. And I'm worried about her."

"Naw. Can't be. You're fibbing. Toads don't get hard-ons."

The Eskridges laughed. "That's a first for science, boys," roared Harge. I can just see a lil' frog-baby hopping about the campfire now!"

"What you going to name it, Milt?" queried Stockton.

"No, no, I didn't *say* she was. I meant I *thought* she was. And it kinda worries me."

"I don't know, fat boy." mused Stockton. "Somehow I just can't picture a frog herding cattle. Cowboys and frog boys don't mix. A toad, yes, since you've proved it could be done. But a frog? Think you could teach your kid frog new tricks, like throwing a loop? Maybe a little branding?"

Everybody was roaring now, and Buchanan too joined in the humor, self-consciously giggling, red-faced and wet-faced. He prayed that the jolliness of the atmosphere would dull Port's kill-crazy temper. He would rather play the clown and live than be a corpse, and sighed in his accepted role.

"Answer me, you tub-o-lard," harshened Stockton suddenly." What you going to name the little frog bastard?"

Buchanan trembled, his prayers for Port's continued humor shattered. "I-I-I think Ralph. Yes, Ralph Buchanan. Ralph is my father back in Missouri, and I think he'd be right proud."

"Ralph?"

"Yes, sir!"

"Naw, not Ralph. Ralph's a man's name. I think it should be Spot. Or Rover."

Fat Bob sat in stony silence, fearful of any reply.

"But nah," continued Stockton. Them's dog's names, and you can't call a toad or a frog or a pollywog by a dog's name. Can you, fat boy?"

Buchanan tried to utter something but the words wouldn't come.

"I'm talking to you, fat-ass," hissed Stockton, leaning toward him with blazing eyes. "I want a fucking answer, and right *now!*"

"Y-Y-Y-Yeah, Port! I mean no!"

"No what?"

"No, you can't call a toad or a frog or a pollywog by a dog's name!"

"And why's that?"

"Uh, uh, because they, they, they—"

"They what?"

"Because they can't bark."

"Really? Well, I want you to bark for me, lard-ass."

"W-w-what?"

"I said bark for me, you fat fuck," ordered Stockton icily.

Milt cleared his throat and forced a light, "Arf!"

"Shit. You can do better than that. Do it, you fat turd. I want some big, manly dog barks."

Buchanan's face poured sweat and he trembled uncontrollably as he squeezed his brain in remembrance of a dog barking. He could hear the others breaking up in uncontrolled laughter, sense Port's volcanic temper on the edge of erupting. He prayed he would not become another notch on Port's gunstock. From his mouth he let out a great "Woof!" Then a second "Woof!"

"More, you fat fucking toad, and *louder!* Go on, give me a bunch!"

"*Woof, woof, woof, woof, woof!*" burst Milt again and again, finding his metier, his imitation barks echoing across the rolling hills and arroyos to the guffawing of his cohorts, but getting confused looks of puzzlement from the cows and horses.

"That's better," grinned Stockton, his reptilian mood slithering away. "From now on when I say 'bark' I want a hefty 'woof' and not an 'arf', got that?"

"Sure, Port, sure."

"Bark!"

"Woof!"

"Bark!"

"Woof!"

"Bark louder, goddamit! Put some manliness and meanness into it!"

"*Woof, woof, woof!*"

"Hey, that's good. Real good. Boys, I want you all to know that we have been a witness to a real freak of nature, a toad that barks!"

Laughter filled the afternoon sun, even from Milt, who was so happy he could cry.

"Bark!"

"*Woof!*"

At the border Stockton sent the others on with the herd. "You boys go on in. You too, fat ass. George and me'll stay here awhile then drop down to my place tomorrow."

Hearing he was off the hook Buchanan was happy as a pig in slop as he loped off with the herd, swimming in euphoric bliss, knowing he would be with his lady-love that night.

In the nippiness of early dawn Woods and Stockton crawled out of their bed rolls to empty bowels and bladders and get a breakfast fire going. They devoured hot cakes smothered with jam and slices of bacon. With coffee to take the chill, they rolled cigarettes and lay back having a relaxing smoke. Peering around the landscape they saw nothing out of kilter, no cows, horses or horsemen to invade their privacy.

"Seems we're pretty safe," uttered Port. "At least up to now. No one trailing our tracks."

"True enough. Probably too early for them to tell what cows they are short of yet."

"Well, whatever, them critters'll all be butchered by evening, and the hides buried."

Stockton stood and began covering the waning fire with his boot-scrapings of sand. "Before we go back I got something to do."

With no questions asked, Woods tightened the cinch of his saddle and climbed aboard. Port had been awful pensive and preoccupied since awakening, and George knew a silent Port was a Port best left alone and unquestioned. Stockton headed south, deeper into Coe country, with Woods nervously following.

Five or six miles later as they were trotting along Stockton revealed what was on his agenda.

"Another few miles, just east of Farmington, is George Coe's ranch. I mean to pay him a long-overdue visit and kill his ass."

Woods didn't care to hear such a dire pronouncement, but was not surprised. Only Port had the gall to ride deep into enemy territory to collect a foe's scalp. He was strangely relieved to hear of it, for at least now he knew what craziness he was going to be a part of, and not kept in the dark or guessing. But it still left him coldly uncomfortable all the way to his bones, feeling he might be riding to his own funeral. Woods made no comment as he rode mutely next to the equally mute and grim-faced Stockton. As they neared their destination and passed a few scattered ranch houses, George hoped they weren't recognized or any alarm was sounded at their presence. Stockton reined up, drew his Colt, injected a sixth shell in the cylinder, and re-holstered the weapon, leaving it rest in the scabbard with the gun free of its hammer-strap. George followed suit, then continued riding alongside Port.

In a short time they slowed to a walk at the base of a low knoll, then stopped altogether amid a small copse of cottonwoods. Before them perhaps a hundred feet away sat a small adobe house with a rafter-covered wooden porch.

"That's Coe's place. Stay here and cover me with your rifle. I'll ride up and 'hello' the cabin. Soon's he show himself I'll drill him. Watch for anybody that might answer fire from inside."

As George slid his Winchester from the boot and chambered a shell quietly into the breech, Port walked his mount slowly forward. Thirty feet from the doorway he stopped and called out, "Hello, the house! Anyone home?"

He hadn't long to wait. George Coe slowly opened the screen door and kept it open with his booted foot. He stood cooly staring at his enemy, cocked pistol casually in hand at his side.

"Why, howdy, Port. What can I do for you?"

Stockton sat with both hands on his saddle horn, irritated that Coe had the edge. His rifle was in its scabbard, loaded and ready, as was his unthonged Colt in its holster. But to try and draw either would be sudden death. Also behind Coe in the shadows was his wife, rifle in hand. The trap he hoped to set fell apart before he could even make a move. Boiling within, he felt a fool.

"Just dropped by wondering if you could use some beef, George," he grinned widely and mirthlessly. "Got some cows be glad to sell you."

"Naw," smiled Coe. "Got all the cows I need this week."

Sarcastic bastard, fumed Stockton. "Dam, George. I was told in town you was in the market for a few head."

"Sorry you made the trip for nothing, Port. You got old news. Or wrong news, anyways."

"Hmmm," mused Stockton aloud, feinting disappointment, eyeing Coe's cocked six-gun at his side. To draw or not to draw, slid the wild thought across Port's fevered brain, wondering if he'd have a lucky day. *Goddam it. This is the worse poker hand I ever drawed to.*

"Guess you're right, George," acceded Stockton. "Done made the trip for nothing."

"Yep. Guess you rightly did."

"Hmmm. Well, 'scuse the bother, George. You take care now," he added with a wave of his hand as he turned and rode off into the trees.

"You do the same, Port," called Coe as he watched the second horseman join him, and the two disappear around the knoll. "Yessiree, Port, you do the same!" he called out with a grin.

On the ride back to his ranch only ten miles eastward Port was a broiling volcano, and not comfortable company to be with. He had been bested and it didn't fit well. George on the other hand felt a great elation and a new lease on life, having been neither a witness to murder, nor involved in a senseless killing.

They looped north and east to avoid settlements of any sort toward Port's small ranch house south of the San Juan River. Along the way it began to snow lightly, and a chilly northern breeze appeared, pushing the flakes south which gradually grew thicker.

At his home they guided their horses into a small barn to leave them with some feed and water, then entered the house.

"Hello, honey," he greeted Emily with a kiss. "George and me are famished to the bone. Hope we got a side of cow left somewheres."

"Sure do. And taters, and gravy, and bisquits, and pie, and coffee, and seconds if you two would like!"

"Good heavens, Emily! I think I'll keep you on here steady!" he laughed, taking her into his arms for a hug.

"Well, I'm glad to hear that, seeing I been looking for a steady job! Now you and George sit and let me fill your plates."

"And let us have some of that good apple cider, sweetheart. It's been a busy day."

George was amazed at the change in Port in Emily's presence. Gone was the sadistic killer, replaced by a bantering, concerned husband. Not an hour ago he was prepared to slaughter Coe with no compunction whatsoever, and now here he was, happy and light hearted in the company of his wife. But George too was happy in her presence, very quietly too, keeping his gaze at her limited to short glances lest his feelings betray him. Sipping their cider and awaiting their meal, Port played with the children, which George couldn't help but notice how calmed the beast was in him. Gone was the widow-maker. After everyone ate, the men sat back a moment having a smoke, gazing out the window at the drifting flakes.

"Have you checked the mail today, honey?"

"No, sweetheart."

"Well, George and me'll go. Give us something to do."

The men rode through the gently swirling flakes the to the post office, housed in the back of a mercantile store in the village of Bloomfield. Entering the building George commented, "While you get

51

your mail I'll pick up some tobacco and makings," and stopped at the counter. As Woods was paying for his purchase there came a sudden shout of curses from the post office area. It was Stockton again, back in his normal heated state.

"Goddam you, Graves! I ought to kill you right where you're standing and be done with it!"

"You leave me be, Port! You got no call to talk to me like that!"

"You bastard! You been calling me a cow thief behind my back, Graves! Well, here I now am, *in* your face! Now call me a thief, c'mon! Do it! Show me what a man you are!"

"I ain't going to do it! Leave me alone, Port!"

"Then step outside right now, you yellow shit! C'mon, so's I can shoot your lying ass!"

The uncontrolled ranting continued for several more minutes until Stockton ended it with, "You low-life coward. I'm leaving now, Graves, but the next time I see you it'll be at the end of my gun when I can shoot you down like the dog you are. So be armed or get your ass outta town!"

Leaving the store the two men returned to the Stockton home, Port in a raging fury. "I'll kill that bastard next time I see him, George! Mark my words! Nobody's going to spread lies about me like that!"

George of course held his silence, wondering at Port's memory of their late expedition of cow gathering. The man-killer was back, and eager as ever to strike.

EIGHT

After several days at the Stockton's, helping with what ranch work had to be done, even chopping up a stack of firewood, Woods left to return to Animas City. It was past the ides of December and turning colder. The forty-mile ride was a nippy one, but with scarf, muffler, gloves, and wrapped in a hefty overcoat, he was fairly comfortable. A slug now and then from his brandy flask was also a great easement. Near the state line about mid-way he halted at a cabin of an acquaintance overnight to escape the drop in temperature.

His short stay with Port and Emily loaned George the internal happiness he sought and needed, for he was at least able to bask in the shadow of the woman he was besotted over. Lamentably, having for so long bathed in the saccharine syrup of his romantic hallucinations, he could no longer summon his brain for logical reasoning. That organ had become clogged from impossible dreams and sluggish from boundless fantasies. It was functioning at quarter-pace, if that, moving slowly with snail-treaded exertion, plodding inch by laborious inch through the thick fen of his perpetual phrenic perversions. Intelligent decision had become ancient history, for he had been ambushed by a strange alchemy making him a prisoner of Eros. There was no turning back. Like the fair-haired Custer not five years before, Woods too was drawn implacably toward his destiny, a helpless pawn of fate. Blinded by a vision only his eyes beheld, he heeded only the enticing call of Circe, and hoped to finally embrace her at the end of his long journey. Consequently, his emotional masochistic state took on a life of its own, demanding iron obedience at every thought of his beloved. Too, playing Port's compadre began to take on a natural role for him, to the point where Port and Emily both turned to him now and then for advice, which to him was no small thing, but an added inner joy of being accepted and trusted, becoming a part of them, and with that thought, a part of her.

There was an incident when Emily stumbled accidently in the kitchen and George was there to quickly reach out and steady her as she wavered in her step. Port was present and admonished her jocosely, "Careful, love, or you'll knock George over!" All three laughed.

But as they did George reeled from the pleasant thrill of his hand for the first time touching forbidden fruit, feeling the press of her breast against his not-so-innocent helping hand. In that fleeting moment he dared to imagine reaching out to embrace her, giving her a quick kiss. His side-long glance of Port's ice-blue orbs gazing upon them gave him cold-shivers and sobered him immediately. It was like suddenly being thrust into a lion's den and he thought he was as good as dead. But Port's kidding words making light of the event gave him a thankful release from terror, and a continued hope for a future with Emily.

Over and over in the weeks to come he repetitiously replayed the kitchen scene in the theater of his mind, giddy at the memory of her warm-nippled breast cupped in his grasp. He also wondered if she recalled the same moment, if she thrilled over it too, and secretly desired George's kiss, and embrace. With that same hand he would sometimes at nights in solitude cup himself privately with frenzied strokes of passion, and with closed eyes see her beneath him again and again as he softly whispered her name,"Emily, Emily, Emily!" and listened to her voice as she crooned his own name, "Oh, George, George, my George!," in echoed passion of love, lust, need and desire, and he would release himself in a tremendous emotional explosion of ejaculation never so deeply experienced, except each time he repeated it. Several times he visited a local whore house to relieve himself in the arms of a purchased woman, but it was no use. He could no more rise to the occasion than fly to the moon. And he also felt guilty in doing so, as if he were betraying his love, for they were not the vessels for him to fill or drink from, for he had become spoken for in his heart and soul to Emily, and cared not to besmirch his feelings for her, or tarnish his great need of her. Yes, he had accepted his severely unspoken loyalty to her in every meaning of the word, but sometimes on rare occasions in moments of dark despair wondered if they were the words of a fool.

NINE

The week before Christmas was a time of celebration for much of the region, and many homes held small parties and get-togethers for friends and relatives alike. Yet, although it was a time for holiday cheer and goodwill to all men, one gathering unknowingly would be the influential fulcrum which would soon dramatically affect the lives of Port Stockton and George Woods. The Francis Hamblets near Farmington threw a dance and supper, inviting a handful of local residents. But alas, before too long, three party-crashers loomed out of the gelid dusk like biblical horsemen of doom, Dyson Eskridge, Jim Garrett and Oscar Pruett. Already having a snootful, they clumped rudely throughout the house, making themselves obnoxious and unwelcome as crashers could be. A Stockton-Eskridge enemy happened to be one of the guests, George Brown, and he sided with his host Hamblet in telling the brash intruders to leave. They did so, but once outside the home the trio commenced shouting and shooting in the night. Brown and Hamblet quickly grabbed their sidearms and exited the house to confront the rowdies. Brown was instantly shot to death. As the melee continued, Pruett was killed next. After this Eskridge and Garrett quickly mounted their horses and fled, riding for Animas City and leaving behind their dead companion.

No time was lost for further retaliatory action, and in Farmington a vigilante group made up of local ranchers was formed to pursue the two gunmen. Unfortunately for Eskridge and Garrett they had small ranches to the north, so in swift vengeance the cluster of horsemen ransacked their homes then burned them to the ground, after which they gathered and took away what stock they could find. Luckily the pair were absent at the time. But when they saw the charred remains of their cabins, they never stopped riding until they reached the safety of Animas City.

Some days later on Christmas night in Marshall's saloon in Durango, George Woods was having some holiday cheer with a crony and Stockton-gang member, Bert Wilkinson. With them in the crowded establishment was Jerry Barthol. The three had been together at the bar for the better part of three hours, matching drink for drink. The five-six and skinny Barthol looked a bit incongruous standing between the pair of six-footers, especially during the last half hour while arguing with Bert. Barthol was incensed over a card game he and Bert were in two months back, and as a result held some sort of grudge.

"God damn it, Jerry!," snapped Bert. "I had a better hand than you, and now you're still pissed over losing. Leave it to hell alone. I don't want to hear another word about it!"

"Well, shit, Wilkinson," retorted Barthol. "I'll settle this in my own way!" And he left in a hot snit.

"Christ, Bert," queried Woods. "What was that all about?"

"Hell if I know, but every time I see him it's the same old crap about me winning a poker hand over him illegally. He's scared to claim I cheated, but keeps saying it was *illegal.* And damn if he'll explain where it was illegal."

"I hear he's a sore loser anyway."

"That's for certain. He can't hardly find a game where he can sit in anymore, and I think that's what irks him."

Barthol quickly ran off to find one of his few friends, Sam "Commanche Bill" Swineford, drawing him into the dispute. After Barthol "explained" things between he and Wilkinson to where Bill felt he had to straighten things out for his friend, he followed Barthol back to Marshall's.

"There he is at the bar, standing next to George Woods," whispered Barthol at the door.

With that Bill swaggered pushingly through the crowd and up to the pair. "Wilkinson, I wants to talk at you."

"Well, hell, Commanche, rave on. Hey, barkeep, get my friend here what he wants. This is George Woods, Commanche. He's an old friend. So, what you want to talk to me about?"

Wilkinson and Commanche were on fairly good terms, and had sat in many a poker game together and shared many a drunk. But now with Barthol spreading poison cleverly enough for the gullible Commanche to bite the bait, he felt the little man was taken advantage of unfairly.

"I just had a talk with my pard Jerry Barthol and he says you screwed him over in a poker game awhile back."

"Oh, Christ, not you too, for heaven's sake. Barthol's a moron, Bill, and you are too, if you believe him."

After that things between the two went from bad to worse, until all one needed was a match to set off the dynamite. Woods just stood wondering why Wilkinson was arguing with such a half-wit, and was beginning to think about leaving. The two men were now shouting back and forth, but so loud was the ruckus throughout the saloon the pair could hardly be heard.

During the heated exchange a duel was strongly suggested by Commanche.

"Well, hell," laughed Wilkinson. "Sure, why not. Choose your weapons."

"Guns," replied Commanche.

"Guns it is," agreed Wilkinson.

"At what distance?" inquired Commanche.

"Right where we stand," answered Wilkinson.

Commanche immediately drew and missed. Bert's bullet caught him in the head, spraying the back bar's bottles and mirror with limited grey matter and blood. The drunken crowd instantly became caught up in the fun of shooting their own guns off and soon the saloon was filled with bullets flying in every direction, including where Bert, Bill and George were standing. Consequently, the already dead Commanche was hit twice more on the way to the floor as Bert and George made their escape.

"Jesus Christ," laughed George on their way to another bar. "Let me have about two minutes head start next time you introduce me to a friend of yours, o.k.? I'd like to at least have a chance to get out of shooting range!"

On the iron-cold late morning of 4 January 1881, seven mounted men from Farmington renewed scouring the countryside for evidence of Dyson Eskridge and Jim Garrett. Hardly ten miles east of town, just south of the San Juan River, in the rolling hills of chamisa country, sat Port Stockton's cabin, nee Ike's. The horsemen approached its vicinity with grave apprehension and caution, knowing of Stockton's cottonmouth temperament and bite. He was not their target, and they planned not to stop, although many of the riders wished his removal. Neither was Port aware yet of the shoot-out at Hamblet's nor the burned-out cabins of Eskridge and Garrett. Yet the riders thought that the two may have stopped briefly to pass on the news of the shooting before running off to Colorado. Either way, at the moment it was "let sleeping dogs lie" as they aimed to cast about for Garrett and Eskeridge, or any other followers of the Colorado group who may be polluting their New Mexico countryside.

The dirt road they were on fronted Stockton's abode about fifty feet, and the chilled, vigilante-ranchers floated by in ghost-like silence. Clouds of steam billowed from the nostrils of horses and men alike, as they kept a wary eye on the cabin with its chimney smoke zig-zagging in the gusty wind. Alfred Graves and Aaron Barker rode point.

Porter was at the kitchen table teaching his young daughters Sarah and Mary how to play checkers when his peripheral vision caught a distant movement through the window. He rose and walked over for a closer look. Riders. Seven. He immediately recognized Graves. The memory of his verbal lashing of him at the post office suddenly set his mind aflame. Confrontational as ever he flew out the door, pipe still in his teeth, drawing his weapon, safety the last thing on his list. He was a timber rattler coiling to strike. Tossing his pipe aside he snarled, "What the hell you bunch of pussies want?!"

Startled, the cluster of horsemen immediately stopped in their tracks as if on cue. The two in the lead, Graves and Barker, turned their horses to face Stockton.

"Stop where the hell you are," warned Port, thumbing the hammer of his Colt.

"Port," spoke Barker, raising his right hand, palm out, as a sign of peace, "we're just riding by and mean you no harm. We've had trouble over at Hamblet's in Farmington just before Christmas. A bad shooting and looking for the men involved, although they probably are up in Colorado by now. Dyson Eskridge and Jim Garrett."

"I don't know nothing about that and don't give a dam neither. I just want you to get the hell off my property and not touch any of my stock."

"We're not stock-hunting, neither, Port," spoke Frank Coe, hoping to cool him down.

"I just bet you ain't, you bunch of goddam maggots! Especially you, Graves. How'd you like to step down and settle up our differences right now? C'mon, you chicken-shit. Try me!"

Stockton was completely out of control and manic. There was no way things were going to be settled peacefully here, thought Barker. Someone's coming out feet first. In the middle of the bunch, Texas gunman Tom Allen Nance surreptitiously slid off his horse and lay a Winchester across his saddle. It was cocked and pointed dead center at Port.

Sarah, ten, and six-year-old Mary stared out the window at what seemed a mime show. Their father howled words they could not hear, words hurled furiously into the wind, as he swung his revolver back and forth for emphasis. They could see it was devilishly gusty with men's scarves and horses manes and tails being blown turbulently. Flakes of snow was thickening too, bouncing and dancing in the growing gale. None of it bothered their father though, gesturing in a hatless and coatless rage, mad over something. The three men in front were getting the most of his verbal attention as he menacingly pointed his cocked Colt at them.

"C'mon, Graves, you yellow piece of cowshit! Get the hell down off that horse and show me what kind of man you are!" Port was a terrifying presence, rabid-eyed and sweeping his gun over the men, practically begging any one of them to make a wrong move.

Port's wife Emily suddenly thrust year-old Carrie into Sarah's arms and sailed out the door.

Nance's rifle cracked its metallic sound throughout the icy afternoon as he drove a bullet into Stockton's chest. Port straightened up jerkily a moment and felt pushed back a step or two as his revolver slipped from his hand. In the sudden silence which surrounded the scene, the posse watched as he crumpled backwards upon the snowy ground. He lay sprawled face up in silence, then straightened out his legs with a soft groan. All the horsemen stared in stunned disbelief, hardly comprehending that Port was actually felled. Suddenly from the house burst Port's wife Emily, rifle in hand, screaming like a banshee, cranking its lever and wildly shooting to beat hell at the knot of men. Everybody was bumping into each other trying to get out of the way; horses startled, stamping and snorting. Graves coolly leaned over with his rifle and snapped a quick shot which hit the stock of Emily's firearm, knocking it out of her hand and sending splinters of wood into her arm and body. Knocked to her knees she raged at the men, "You goddam ball-less bunch of white trash! Go away, you bastards! Go away and leave us in peace! You all done what you come here for, now go on home and tell your wives and children what brave men you are!"

The vigilantes sheepishly turned and wordlessly retraced the way they had come. Emily cradled and rocked her husband's cooling body in her bloody arms under the falling snow.

"Oh, Port honey, please don't go!"

"Emily," he sighed, hardly breathing. "Oh, God, it hurts."

"Please Port, you'll be okay, I know you will!" she pleaded, rocking him back and forth. "Oh, husband, please stay! Tell me you will!"

"Ohhh, mama, mama, help me. It hurts so bad, I can't breathe." And with a brief trembling sigh he was dead.

Sarah and Mary stared out the window at their mother rocking their father's lifeless body. Little Carrie baby-talked gibberish as she too was rocked gently in Sarah's arms. The two girls stood trembling and frightened, their faces wet with silent tears. They wondered if all they saw was real. It was a haunting experience which would follow them forever.

TEN

Ike, having left the previous November for Texas with several of the gang to pick up a herd of hot cattle, was still on the trail when Port was killed. On a mid-January afternoon he was at the head of 500 shuffling cows approaching the house when he sighted George and Emily standing on the porch. He uncomfortably sensed something was amiss the moment he saw Emily's right arm completely wrapped in white from shoulder to hand, and in a sling.

"Good lord, Emily," he inquired with a frown. "That don't look too comfortable. What in the world happened?"

"Afraid we have some bad news, Ike," revealed George, as he went on to describe the shoot-down of Port and Emily's wounding.

"Those rotten bastards," growled Ike. "I'll kill every one of them murderers, or die trying."

"I'm really sorry, Ike, and wish I'd of stayed on longer instead of going back to Animas City. But when I heard what happened I come back real quick to make sure Emily was all right. Been helping tend her since."

"Glad you did, George. How's that arm, Emily? Did you take a bullet?"

"No. The bullet hit the gunstock and splintered, sending wood into my arm and side."

"So who shot you? Did you recognize him?"

"Alf Graves. Port had a fight with him at the post office a few days before."

"Graves? I'll surely get him for this. Who was it got Port?"

"Tom Nance. He shot from behind a horse. Others was George Lockhart and Frank Coe." And I remember Burr Milleson and Al Dustin. And Aaron Barker."

"Six more to keep me busy. Where's Port buried?"

"Out front," she pointed. "Just across the road."

Ike rode toward the fresh-painted white wooden marker sixty-some feet away, Woods behind him and afoot. At the mound of dirt he dismounted and removed his hat. Standing before the cross he asked, "Who buried him, George?"

"Me and Bert Wilkinson. Really wish I could of been more help, Ike," he self-consciously re-apologized.

Ike stood in silent preoccupation, shaking his head slowly. "Dammit, Port. Dammit to hell." His eyes misted and he didn't bother to wipe them. He was caught up in a thousand thoughts, half of them questions, the other half burning with revenge. "We got to find out everybody in that posse and kill every one of them, George. Ain't no other way I'm going to settle this."

George genuinely had no desire to play anybody's avenging angel, but he let that disloyal thought lay undisturbed in the back of his mind. He saw no sense in riling Ike in his present state, nor have him inflict any wrath his way because of him holding an alien judgement. But having a vivid imagination he could nervously hear the sounds of many echoing shots and see the potential of a large body-count.

Stockton replaced his hat and walked his horse, reins in hand, back to the house. Woods mutely followed.

"George, I'd like you to stay and tend to Emily, if that's okay by you?"

"Sure. All right. No problem at all."

"No way I can leave this herd here we just brought in, not with the Farmington bunch on the prod now. Me and the boys'll run them up to Animas City to pasture where they'll be safe. We also got a lot of re-branding to do. Port's got forty-some cows you can watch over for now, but keep your eyes open. We'll keep dropping in now and then to see how things are. If anything needs our quick attention, get word to us quick."

Early next day, with Emily at his side, George watched from the porch as the last of Ike's herd moved out for Colorado, Emily beside him. The days had been somewhat mild, pleasantly easing the bite from the icy nights. The sunny afternoons appeared as a portent to him, of a lift in his life toward better things. Here he was with Emily now, all he had ever hoped and wished for, just he and her together with their future ahead of them, a golden road to share hand in hand. He turned to look at her. She had been so quiet and withdrawn all this time, since Port's killing. The shock had done something to her mind. The shooting of her and the rifle butt shards exploding into her body while she was pumping slugs at the posse, screaming like a wild woman, both of them on the ground, and finally taking Port in her arms as he died must of been a gruesome experience. Now it was like she had given up on her life. He wanted to wrap his arm around her, give her solace, hope and love. There was a grief in her he desired to erase.

"Em?"

She stood in silence, staring at the empty space the cows had disappeared into.

"How's your arm? Getting better now?"

"Some," she replied indifferently. "I'll be glad when this sling's off."

"Tomorrow's when we go to Bloomfield so the doctor can remove the bandages."

"I know. That'll be a blessing."

"You'll feel good when all that is off you. Like shedding a burden."

"That's for certain."

She was so fragile to look at, having lost a lot of weight. So small, remote and distant. The hell she had been put through only she could describe, and all he could think of was to hold her and protect her. For the first time since he had been living here, taking care of her and the kids, sleeping on the front room floor on a bundle of blankets, he took a chance and slid his arm around her to pull her gently toward him. To clasp her just once, as he had wanted to when he first saw her, only once. As his arm curled lightly around her shoulder he turned with yearning to take her into his embrace, anticipating the melting warmth of her surrender. But she froze and stepped back, gently pressing her left hand against his chest.

"No, George. Please. I appreciate all you've done for me and the children, and I do thank you. You're such a good man. But I can't. Not now. Please."

"Uh, I'm sorry, Em. I didn't mean it to look like I was grabbing at you. But you seem so hurt inside I just wanted to hold you a minute, to comfort you."

"Oh, George, you're so sweet and kind. And with all you've done for me and the young 'uns. Please don't ever think I'm ungrateful. But don't you worry, I'll be fine. I surely will."

"No, no, I understand, Em. I do."

But Emily's rebuff was like a splash of cold water, and he prayed his move hadn't alienated her from him completely. Yet, what else could he do to demonstrate his feelings for her? Talk had never been his strong suit in the game of romance, and he had never felt this way before in his life. The few flings he had had were of a sexual nature, several young things over the years who were as willing and ready as he to fall into bed to sate a lustful attraction, or maybe the business bargain of a few cathouse couplings. But love? My God, it was a strange, wondrous roller-coaster ride of the emotions! A strange country indeed! And now this time her spurning him plunged his roller-coaster into the darkness of rejection. How harsh a cut it was, the sudden knife-thrust to his heart after the joy he was feeling. *Oh, my poor Emily! I did not mean to embarrass you or turn you away! I promise to mend things.* Yes. He would be more patient and kind.

The seven-mile wagon drive eastward the next day to the doctor in Bloomfield was under a pleasant wintery sky, the temperature in the mild 50s. But conversation remained stilted and static. George did the best he could to make things light and sociable, jabbering of cows, cattle, horses and ranching in general. Emily was non-committal and outwardly friendly, yet still distant and not very communicative. No matter how he tried, George could not bring back the old Emily of their previous trip from Animas City, when she was laughing and bubbly and so carefree, so filled with life. Perhaps she would never come back from where she had now buried herself, feeling safer now within a fortified self, after the shock of having Porter practically murdered in her arms. George despaired at his inept social graces, at his inability to even draw a smile from her poker expression, and in his own dark self wondered if he were to kill Alf Graves for the damage he surely had done to her, self-defense or not, she would be able to not only smile again, but smile at him.

Driving down the main dirt street of town and following its half-muddy and partially snow-covered ruts, he pulled up to the rack before the doctor's office, dismounted, and tied up. Walking around to Emily's side he saw in pleasant surprise she had awaited him to help her down. "Easy, now, Em, though it seems pretty dry from here on in." Once on the ground she let him lead her with his hand on her elbow to the boarded walk.

"Thank you, George. I'm afraid I still feel a bit wobbly."

Once inside, George doffed his hat and in a moment the nurse was at their side, expecting them. "Oh, Emily, and how is that arm fairing?" she inquired.

"Just fine, Edith, and I can hardly wait to get these bandages off. Much of the soreness is gone, really!"

"Well, let me tell the doctor you're here. You sit and make yourself comfortable."

Only one other person was in the office, and he rose to walk over to George. "Why, hello, George," he smiled. "Good to see you!"

"Well, Joel Estes! It surely has been a long time. How in the world are you?"

"Just fine. Had to pick up some medicine for the kids. A couple of them have colds and are sniffling till I'm about crazy." Joel Estes Jr. was a widower with six children.

"Em, this is my good friend, Joel Estes. Joel, my friend Emily."

"Why, pleased to meet you, maam," Joel greeted, extending a large hand. He too was a tall man, extending over six feet to match George in height, although a few pounds more muscle. "I see your arm is a bit incapacitated," he grinned mightily, "and I do hope George isn't taking advantage of you in arm-wrestling contests?"

"Oh," she laughed. "Come to think of it, he rudely *does* love to show off his strength."

"George, you rascal, you taking advantage of this tiny damsel has come to an end. And at this very moment too, by golly, or we will have to make a journey to the woodshed. I'll have no more of this!"

George, taken aback, could but stutter at the sudden easy exchange between Joel and Emily as if they had known each other for years. Too, her light laughter and sparkling eyes had miraculously returned as she traded repartee with his friend. The nurse Edith appeared and informed her the doctor was ready.

"It was nice meeting you, Emily," grinned Joel warmly as he extended his hand again. "I hope we'll see each other again."

"So do I," she chimed. "It was pleasant talking to you. And I hope the medicine helps your children's colds."

Woods walked out the door with Estes, grateful for the reacquaintance. "So how's your farm getting along, Joel?"

J. S. Peters

"Busy, George, Busy. Got another batch of hogs and cows in the other day, and what with the goats, sheep, horses, chickens and rabbits—not to mention the garden. Sleep keeps getting in my way."

Estes ran a hugely productive farm and produce business near Farmington and was quite successful, having a natural affinity for the trade.

"Sounds like you could use another hand, maybe."

"Certainly could, by golly. Hell, you were a good hand whenever you worked for me in the past George, and I'd welcome the chance to hire you anytime, if you have a mind to do so."

"Good. Glad that's settled, I could use a job. I'll come out Monday next week, O.k.?"

"That'd be good. I'll be looking for you. I hear you been taking care of the Port Stockton place. That won't interfere with your time with me, will it?"

"No, no. Guess you done heard of Port being killed?"

"Yes, I have, and a real shame, even mean as he was. Never knew him, but recall seeing him once in Durango with Emily. Sweet little thing, and couldn't understand her yoking herself up with him one bit. How's she taking everything with what happened, being wounded and all?"

"She's been quiet and broody a lot, but that's the first time since before the shooting I seen her smile and laugh and jabbing away so lightful as with you in the office."

"Well, I could see her face was awful long and thought I'd try and joke her out of herself, you know? Can't take yourself too seriously too long, is my motto."

"Guess you're right there."

"So, ah, you and her taking to each other in ways permanent?"

"Oh, no, Joel! I like her an awful lot, surely, but no, I just sleep on the front room floor and am like a working hand, you know? Ike asked me when he come back from Texas to stay until she got on her feet, and to watch the stock. I done spent all my savings keeping her and the kids together in food and needs, you know?"

"Listen, George, I hear you been doing a good job dog-watching the place, and a lot of people respect you for it, although they can't figure your friendship with the Stockton people. And that's none of my business anyway, cause you've always been straight with me in all our dealings. But if you two people could use some vittles, just ask."

66

"That's good of you, Joel, but—"

"Hell, never mind the 'but', c'mere." Estes pulled Woods by the arm to the back of the wagon parked next to his. Reaching in, Estes pulled wrapped packages of various meats and bags of produce and lay them into the bed of Woods' vehicle. "And here's a sack of spuds, some cabbage, carrots, melons. And oh, yes, spinach, corn, cucumbers."

"Good lord, Joel, that's enough for an army!"

"Sure is. Couldn't sell it all this trip, so feast up. What with growing kids, this stuff 'll be gone in an hour," he laughed.

Just then Emily appeared, arm free of its trappings and sling.

"Well, looky here," Estes observed in mock amazement. "Hardly recognized you without your wrappings, Miss Emily!"

"That is one article of clothing I will never miss, thank you!" she smilingly reported. "And what in the world is all them packages and things doing in the back? George, you been shopping?"

"Er, I," he sputtered.

"No, maam, it's all my fault. Since this is a holiday I figured this would be a good way to celebrate."

"Holiday?" puzzled Emily.

"Yep," retorted Estes. "We are celebrating the removal of all them entanglements you were a prisoner of. And you certainly look a lot more fetching without them, maam."

"Why thank you, Mister Estes," beamed Emily. "And in return George and I would like to invite you for dinner to equally celebrate your most kind gesture."

"And I most happily accept the invite, Miss Emily. Yes sirree, I sure do!"

Soon, dinners with guest-neighbor Joel Estes became a natural and common event, with Joel bringing various meats and foodstuffs on each trip. In fact, the month of February found Estes on their doorstep so often it seemed he was a resident. Each time he appeared Emily would light up like a Christmas tree, and the three girls would dance around in glee as if he were Santa, for he never failed to bring each of them something. Many afternoons Joel would take them for a ride, weather permitting, to Bloomfield for a candy treat or ice cream for the children. Woods accompanied them the first two excursions but bowed out thereafter, reading the writing on the wall. Estes was obviously courting Emily, and she more than obviously welcomed his attention and presence like an eager teenager. A half-dozen times he took them to his farm for the day, giving them a tour of his extensive operation, where the kids cavorted with the goats, sheep and dogs. Whenever together the two were happy and smiling and couldn't keep their eyes off each other or do enough for the other. Sometimes from the corner of his eye George would catch Joel slipping his arm around Emily's waist to pull her hip gently against him, and he would ache at the sight remembering his own rejected attempt at putting his arm around her shoulders at what seemed so long ago. They had fallen in love, it was obvious, and George felt like the biggest third wheel in the county.

Yet while heart-broken at what he knew what was taking place from the first moment the two met in the doctor's office hardly a month before, he was happy for them. He also knew, and it was difficult for him to admit, that she would soon leave and there would be a void in his life forever. But what could he expect? he asked his realistic self. What did he have to offer her? She was a widow with three young girls to raise, and she knew he was only a part-time carpenter, herder, and some-time rustler for Ike. Joel was a solid, hard working farmer with nothing but a good economic future ahead of him. Emily at one time may have been the faithful wife of a gunfighter on the run much of the time, living a hand-to-mouth existence, but that was no comparison to the life Estes could offer her now. Port was ancient history, and so how could she look upon George with any favor? But damn! Didn't she know how much he cared for her? As much or even more than Joel! He knew he could probably get steady work in Durango with all their building. He wished he had approached her earlier, more forcefully, explained his feelings and made plans with her, but naw, it was too late now. It was a bitter meal for him to digest, for he knew that after all was said and done it was the reality that she was deeply in love with Joel. All the jobs in the state he could garner for himself would not matter a hill of beans. Aw, the hell with it.

Coming in from the barn early dusk one evening Woods was surprised at welcome smells from the kitchen. As he opened the door his heart leaped as he saw Emily setting platters of food on the table, thinking his day with her had finally come. She and her daughters lately took to staying several days at Estes' farm. She sometimes left the children there, where they begged to stay, glad to do chores for Joel.

"Why, hello, Em," he welcomed in repressed excitement. "Didn't know you were back."

"Hello, George. Well, the kids wanted to stay so I let them, knowing they'd be fine. I put some steaks on, hoping you'd be hungry enough for them."

"Oh, sure," he grinned. "I could probably do a bang-up job on a whole cow right now."

"Well, good. And I got everything with them you like."

Quickly washing his hands and face in the kitchen, he sat at the table while she placed a piece of beef on his plate. He helped himself to the boiled potatoes, gravy, string beans, fried bread and butter as she poured them coffee. He sliced a chunk of the steak, and after he chewed and swallowed most of it said, "Oh, Em, this is most divine! Your cooking gets better with every meal!"

"Thank you, George."

They ate mostly in silence, exchanging a word here and there of non-importance, until Woods had to ask the hated question. He just had to know if his prayers were answered. "Will you be moving soon, Em?"

"Pretty soon, George," she replied solemnly but firmly.

His heart sank. "Well, honestly, Em. I'm glad it's Joel you're going to. He's a good friend and you sure couldn't pick a better man."

"Oh, George, I'm so glad you feel that way! He makes me so happy!"

"I know. It shows in you every day."

"And the girls take to him too, and that's a mighty blessing."

"Yes, it surely is. Important as all get-out."

There was a clumsy pause as they continued cutting and chewing, conversation about played out. After a long moment Emily looked across at him and said, "We're getting married next week, George. Twelfth of March."

Oh, God! he thought. "Oh, Em, that's good! Really good to hear!"

"And we're having a big wedding party and dance two days later in Farmington. We want you to come. You will, won't you?"

"Really?" he smiled. "Well, I'll surely be there, I will!"

ELEVEN

Ike Stockton, disdaining with scorn the reports of a $2,000 bounty for him by the Farmington fraternity, boldly dropped down upon the New Mexico pastureland to gather up what cattle could be found of Eskridge and Garrett's. He took with him Garrett, Tom Radigan, Charlie Allison, Gus Hefferon and a trio of others. But the small herds were delinquent, having been adopted by the same arsonists who left both men's cabins in gutted piles of ashes. Near the sight of Garrett's charred abode the men camped and put up a portable tent.

"They done a bang-up job on your cabin there, Jim," commented Stockton. "Matches Dyson's like a twin."

"Damn sure does," muttered Garrett. "And I'd like to return the compliment, with interest."

"We'll get our chance. Don't you worry."

"Can't be soon enough to suit me."

The following afternoon, after finishing off a late lunch from a butchered calf of their foes, the group refilled their cups with a last cup of coffee and a cigarette before striking the tent.

"You closing up Port's place?" queried Garrett of Ike.

"Yeah. I'll have George drive Port's cows up to pasture with these. But we'll still use Port's cabin as a line camp whenever we're in the vicinity doing a collection."

"Or til they burn that out too," added Dyson sourly.

Just then over a low knoll and through the brush a short distance off appeared a pair of riders trotting toward their encampment in tandem. In moments they recognized each other. The two men were Aaron Barker and Tom Nance, and to Ike, known executioners of his brother.

They had unwittingly stumbled across the Stockton men not realizing who they were, and were as surprised as they. At the edge of the camp Barker slid to a stop and jumped from his horse snapping off a shot from his six-gun. He hit Radigan in the knee, which he would later lose via amputation. The camp then came alive with a fusillade of shots. Ike quickly disposed of Barker with a rifle shot to his body, then killed his mount with a shot to its head. Nance, several horse-lengths away, stopped to do a bit of target practice himself with his own sidearm, but seeing things were not in his favor with the odds at seven-to-one, wisely swerved his steed about and raced back toward Farmington.

"God damn it," shouted Stockton, "let's get him!"

Within seconds Stockton was in the saddle and off like the wind giving pursuit, followed by his cohorts. He knew Nance was the one who had shot Port, and now this was his chance. But Nance was known for both, first-class horseflesh and first-class gun work, and his steed easily loped away from the chasers, outdistancing them in moments. Far ahead as he was, he would stop and turn about a moment to snap off a shot or two at his pursuers from his Winchester as if in cool amusement. At these moments, aware of Nance's reputation as a dead shot, the men would slow up a moment and hug their mount's necks to avoid a possible bullet, and nervously realize too, that their horses made excellent targets. Then, as Nance turned to continue his ride with a coarse laugh, the three would kick their horse's flanks again, hoping to get close enough for a few shots, or that with luck Nance's mount would stumble. But Nance had a sure-footed stallion and was also smart enough to keep out of rifle range. After about five miles Nance did some serious riding and pulled away from his prey as if they were standing still. The pursuers quit, not wanting exhausted mounts so near their enemies haunts. They were getting too close to Farmington and decided to quit while they were ahead.

"Well, shit,"oathed Stockton. "We'd best get back and move that herd. We don't want an army of them bastards to face."

"Ain't that the truth,"agreed Eskridge.

"Sure would love to have Nance's horse," admired Garrett. "Wonder where in hell he stole it?"

"Most likely a Texas export," laughed Eskridge. "Let's ask him next time we run into him. Maybe he'll give the address."

"Both of you are crazy," chuckled Stockton. "Let's make tracks while we can!"

The Stockton men with satisfaction settled up the debt of their two members cow and cabin losses by collecting fifteen of Lacy's horses and four hundred cattle from Lacy and Cox.

TWELVE

The Estes' post-wedding dinner-dance was a well-attended affair. The only thing that dampened it for Woods was the sight of Milt Buchanan as one of the guests. Moving about the rooms in scattered conversation with a handful of people he knew, he learned Buchanan was a new employee of Estes, hired just the day before. George never ran into him because he himself had quit Estes under the pretense of soon moving to Durango for a construction job, and since Ike decided to abandon the house he had vacated earlier for Port and Emily. Woods was to run the cattle up to Animas City, and the house would be used by the gang whenever they meandered through the vicinity doing "field work." George was tempted to stay on working for Joel, but thought better of it knowing that sooner or later his feelings for Emily would eventually ruin his friendship for Estes, by overriding his good sense to leave well enough alone. Being too close to his emotions yet, he could just look upon Emily and melt. No, he had best go.

In the meantime he'd just socialize and avoid Buchanan, then leave before an hour was up, right after treating himself to the sumptuous banquet table. He wanted no trouble with the fat man, at least not here. Now and then Woods would spy him across the room holding court with several cronies as Buchanan snickered and nodded toward Woods. This is when he was tempted to walk over and ask him what in hell was so funny. George knew he was most likely spreading garbage, for that was his game, to operate in the background with invented inferences and false rumors. Several times he saw him speaking briefly with Estes, and dreaded what the vicious bastard was saying. Woods in turn over the evening chatted a few times with Estes, and he couldn't help but notice a coolness from him each time. After eating a plate of selected items, Woods decided to leave and looked about for his host to say his goodnights. He spotted Joel among a knot of men, one of them Buchanan. Good. He wished to hear whether the fat man had any parting words of wisdom for him, and then he would . . . . No, he corrected himself. Not here. Yet Woods was feeling edgy, had been all evening, and it was so unlike him. Repressed anger was growing within him and he couldn't quite get a grip on why. Probably it was Buchanan with his smug smirks and nods tossed his way that ate at him. Well, maybe so, but he wasn't going to let it get to him. Woods walked over to Estes with an easy grin and palm outstretched.

"Joel, thanks for the fine evening. And I wish you and Emily the best."

Ignoring the proffered hand, Estes looked upon him as if he were a stranger. "Oh, really? I thought you had left after you filled your gut."

"Now, Joel," puzzled Woods. "Why in the world would you think that?"

"Hell, I been feeding you like a king the past month," in reference to his food deliveries to the Port Stockton ranch.

"But Joel, that was for all of us which you insisted on, and we all thanked you for your kindness."

"Never mind kindness, George. I also don't appreciate what things you have said, either."

"What things?" he asked, looking at the four other men's faces, wondering what was going on. "I don't know what you're talking about, Joel. I honestly don't."

"Maybe we should settle this outside, like men."

"Settle what?"

"You know what in hell I mean."

"But I don't, honestly. And no way I want to have a fight with you. You're my friend, Joel. Can't we talk about whatever it is?"

"Ain't nothing I want to talk about. Talk would be a waste."

"I'm leaving, Joel. I don't know what's happened, but good night. And I sincerely do wish you and Emily the best."

Estes himself turned and walked into the large front room where dancers were busily moving about to the sounds of a pair of fiddles, guitar and clarinet.

Woods depressingly entered a back room set aside for guests' belongings, strapped on his pistol belt, donned his hat and shrugged into his heavy winter coat. Feeling terrible, Woods knew something was inferred or said about him and Emily to set Joel on the warpath. It had to have been Buchanan spreading his poison, who else? My God, he loved Emily, and still did, and would never cross the line with her in any way. Protecting her all that time, lord, he would have killed for her! He was strictly like a hired hand, sleeping on the floor, taking care of them all best he could, and Joel of course constantly giving them groceries helped a hell of a lot. That was more than kind of him, although he was certainly thinking of Emily in a courtship sort of way. But so what? He didn't blame him, he would have done the same. And he had spent all his savings on them during that time, all $135. Too, when the wedding was set he gave Joel his good suit for the wedding since he didn't have one and they wore the same size. They had been good friends two years, and now it was shot to hell. Yes, it had to have been from the lying mouth of Buchanan.

As Woods left the room he came face-to-face with the fat man in the hallway. Instantly boiling over at his foe's insolent sneer, George grabbed a bunch of shirtfront with his left fist and with his right drew his six-gun, shoving the barrel up and under his chin. Slowly thumbing back the hammer, the four metallic clicks echoed in both men's ears.

"You slimy turd," Woods rasped, eyes enraged. "I just know it was your flappy mouth that set Joel against me. You filthy, rotten scum."

"P-p-please, George! I know we got our differences, but—arrggh!" he choked in pain as Woods jammed the barrel higher.

"Shut up damn you! Or I'll finish what Port should of done long ago!"

"Okay, okay, I'm sorry! I truly am, honest!"

"From now on I don't want to hear another word of insult from your stupid mouth, understand? And if I ever hear of you spreading any of your crappy-ass lies about me behind my back, you're as good as dead. Got it?"

"Y-y-yes, George! I won't never! I promise!"

Shaking and sweating in terror, the fat man's intestines and bladder surrendered their contents, releasing all in a descending deluge.

"Phew, fat ass. Smells like you done let all that food you stuffed yourself with run down your legs. Better go wipe yourself and refill your stomach."

Woods shoved away the waste-drenched Buchanan, re-holstered his Colt, and departed.

THIRTEEN

George looked up at the sound of thumping hooves in the sandy soil one afternoon to see Burt Wilkinson and Harg Eskridge cantering off the trail and into the front yard.

"Well, you two are a welcome sight," greeted Woods. "Haven't had a soul out here in near three weeks."

"Good to see you, George," grinned Burt. "Hope you have a steak or two available."

"You bet. Climb down and come on in. What's new?"

"Ike sent us down to help bring in Port's cows," spoke Harg. "Thought it was about time before the Farmington bunch gets any more nasty ideas."

"Suits me. Don't mind saying I've had more than a few nervous nights waiting for something unwelcome to happen."

"We'll load up the wagon this afternoon," added Harg. "Then move out first thing in the morning."

"Good. Ain't too much gear to take, but one wagon load sounds about right."

"First let's feast down some chow," exclaimed Burt. "I got to eat a decent meal before I drop."

"Yessiree," agreed Harg. "I hear you turn out a good side of beef, George. I'd like to check out that rumor right about now."

"O. k., you're on!" laughed Woods. "While you two unsaddle and water them beasts I'll start burning the cow-hide."

The meal with company was a welcome break for Woods, and the good news of finally moving the small herd away from potential disaster was a godsend. "So what's the latest from up in Colorado?" he inquired over the table.

"There's been a few shootings," answered Eskridge as he chewed hungrily. "But nothing special unless you're the one being shot."

"Anyone I know?"

"Let's see," pondered Harg. "Only one worth mentioning is a scrap of sorts at the Coliseum Theater in Durango. Tom Lynch and Jack Roberts with their girl friends Mabel and Alice got into a drunken disagreement and started whipping each other. Then a bystander, Tom Greatorex, sticks his nose in to help one of the women like a true gentleman and Jack smacks him on the head with his six-gun, dropping him to the floor. As he tried to get up Jack finishes the job by pumping a bullet into him, terminating his knightly behavior."

"I remember Greatorex," mused Woods. "Always playing the rescuer. Decent man, but not too savvy."

"After that,"continued Harg, "the marshall steps in and Jack also clobbers him a couple times with his gun, knocking him down and out. Jack then leaves the show and gallops out of town."

"Well," sighed Woods. "As much as I'm bored out here with these speechless cows, maybe I shouldn't complain so much after all."

"And that ain't the end of it," added Eskridge. "Jack made it down to Colorado near Farmington where to his misfortune he was grabbed by Tom Nance and John Benning. Because of a reward they sent a friend to Durango notifying the sheriff that if he comes down with the money they'll turn him over. The sheriff wastes no time and gallops down with the reward and a dozen assistants and pays off Nance. On the way back the posse holds a horse-back court, and it seems about four miles out of Durango they couldn't endure passing up another tree, so hanged him."

"Jack was too unsociable and was a bad drunk, anyway," injected Burt. "Many's the time in his cups he pissed off not too few with his mouth."

"Amen to that," agreed Harg. "Pour me some more of that good coffee, George."

The men sat quiet for a time, picking their teeth and complimenting Woods over his cooking.

"George," inquired Eskridge, "what's this I hear of you shoving a gun in Buchanan's face?"

"Uh, aw," embarrassed Woods. "Wasn't anything. Just a minor disagreement of sorts."

"Not from what we heard," added Wilkinson. "Also Joel Estes was on to you about something. You ain't got a feud going on, have you?"

"No, no, no! It's like I said, just a small dispute."

"Well, now," continued Eskridge. "Can't be too small with fat-boy saying how he wants your scalp."

"Oh, hell, he's all talk, you know that."

"Yes he is," commented Harge. "But I'd watch my back with that one. I can't understand how he's managed to live so long. He's long way past his life expectancy."

"I do believe," said Wilkinson, "that Port was ready to do him in, being tired of clowning around with him. About a month ago one night I had to slap him side of the head with my gun to remind him to mind his manners. Seems like he never learns."

"Would you believe," chuckled Eskridge, "that he actually thinks he's a romantic danger around women?"

"You're right about that!" laughed Burt.

"Listen, George," confided Harg. "Fat-boy runs his mouth about Port's widow, Emily, mainly because he's jealous of what he imagines did or did not take place while you were guarding this ranch."

"Now damn it, fellas!" protested Woods archly. "Let's be clear about that right here and now. She and I had absolutely nothing to do with each other. And that's the truth!"

"Hey, easy now, George," replied Harg, both hands raised palms up toward Woods. "We believe you, we really do. And whatever happened or didn't happen is nobody's business in the first place anyway. I know you're a good and honest man, George, but people will still talk. It's human nature. What's unbearable at times are the intentional lies, gossip and insinuations some people spread out of envy, or just plain nastiness. Like fat-boy."

"To be frank," grunted Woods, "I did have a few words with Buchanan, shoving my Colt up under his chin to emphasize my point. I felt like a fool afterwards, but you know how it is in the heat of things. I hope to never lose my head like that again."

"Just a week ago," Eskridge went on, "he made a snotty remark about you and Emily and I back-handed him off the Animas bridge into the river. I stood and watched him yell and sputter and flounder like a squealing whale, hoping he'd drown. And do you know he actually made it to the bank and crawled out? It was unbelievable!"

That's when I figured God had something special in store for him down the road."

"Whatever it is,"groused George. "I hope I'm there to witness it."

"Georgie boy," chuckled Eskridge. "You ain't heard the latest."

"What's that?"

"Hold on to your britches. Ol' fat-boy Buchanan done got his lady-love in the family way."

"Whaat?" amazed Woods. "She's really pregnant?"

"Yep. Five months worth."

"Think it's his?"

"Has to be," spoke Burt. "Ain't a human male within a thousand miles would mate with that ugly hog. Can you picture them two sows going at it?"

Roaring with tears running down his face Harg injected, "Would that be called a ceremony or a ritual?"

"More a miracle!" howled Burt.

Wilkinson and Eskridge were lost in such riant laughter it left them weak and wet-faced. Woods could only shake his head and smile at the two as they went half out of control at Buchanan's expense.

"Oh, Christ!" panted Harg, getting his breath. "I ain't had such a belly laugh in years. Feels almost as good as getting laid."

"Damn if it don't" echoed Burt.

"Well, I wish them all the luck in the world," surrendered Harg. "Never know about a thing like that. It just might straighten out fat-boy enough to make him passably tolerable."

"You could be right," agreed Burt.

After another round of coffee they cleared the table and helped George clean up the plates and kitchen. They then cleared the house and barn of gear and items to be taken back to Animas City in the wagon. It was near sunset when they finished.

"Lets have another pot of George's good coffee and play a little poker before calling it a night," suggested Eskridge.

"Good idea," answered Wilkinson. "And to make it friendly, let's play for chips and no money."

"I second that," came Woods. "Since I'm busted anyway."

"Suits me fellas," came Harg's reply, with a stretch and a yawn.

It wasn't too long into the game before Woods ruefully saw that his luck in cards was no better than his luck in romance. The entire two hours they played was a downer for him, for Lady Luck shat on him all night. Of course it was his inability to concentrate on the game. Much as he looked forward to the move from New Mexico he just couldn't divorce himself from the constant thoughts of Emily. His three weeks of solitude certainly didn't free him any, and the nights were torture. During this last week he felt he finally had a handle on his head and heart, in that a numbness subtly grew over him like a crab's shell, something he thought of as a defense against danger, or a vaccination against poison. Maybe time worked like an inoculation. But no matter how comfortable in his solitude he felt he was becoming, all day long, whether working in the barn or pasture, he caught himself occasionally glancing westward, hoping for the sight of Emily and the kids in the wagon calling and waving to him. Back they would soon be. Forever. In his mind.

Now with the company of Wilkinson and Eskridge he hoped the men's presence would take him away from his perpetual moping and endless day-dreaming. But no, company without her was no company at all.

"George?" came Burt's voice.

"Huh? What?"

"I said, how many cards do you want?"

"Oh, yeah. Let's see . . . ."

"You're awful busy in the head," replied Burt. "That's the third time I asked you."

"Sorry. Just tired, I guess."

"So? How many?"

George stared at his hand as if awakening to the fact he was playing poker. Three clubs, two diamonds. Was his luck about to change? Quietly elated he discarded the two and six of diamonds.

"I'll take two."

"Harg?" asked Wilkinson.

"I'll take two."

After dealing Eskridge's cards he quipped, "Hell, no use changing horses. I'll take two myself."

George stared at the three clubs in his hand; king, queen, jack. His drifting mind equated them to his late dilemma. Emily sat in his fist pressed between suitors: king Joel, queen Emily and jack George. He felt like a king once. Now he had been removed from the throne, deposed. He was a common jack, now. A knave in the deck of life. A jackass.

"I'm raising the pot fifty dollars," announced Harg with a smug smile.

George drew the pair off the table and slipped them behind his hand. Recklessly, without looking, he tossed in fifty in chips and added nonchalantly, "Fifty more, big fella."

"Jesus, George," blurted Wilkinson. "You mean you finally got a decent hand?"

"Hell, Burt," retorted Harge. "He ain't even looked at his down cards. He's bluffing."

"Maybe so," lamented Burt. "But a hundred big ones? No way I can even call with this garbage," and he threw his hand in.

George squeezed one of his two new cards to peek at slowly in masochistic expectation. To complete his flush he needed a pair of clubs. Even the joker would help, good for aces, straights or flushes. On the edge of the card he slowly slipped out he saw, oh my God! Finally fully exposing the corner he saw the joker, good as a ten or ace of clubs. A royal flush was nearly his! But even a ten or ace of any other suit would give him a high straight, not too shabby a hand. Better yet, a lowly deuce of clubs would give him a low flush.

"C'mon, George," egged Eskridge. "What you want to do?"

"Huh?"

"I just raised another fifty."

"Oh, I'll raise your fifty."

"But hell, you ain't looked at your last card."

"Lady Luck is finally at my side, Harg."

"I think she's leading you astray, 'ol buddy. And oh, how I wish this was cash!"

"Yeah, me too," agreed George. "I could sure use it."

"All right, stop all this yammering and stalling and get with it. I'm raising your fifty. Now, you want to look at that last card before betting? Or throw away your chips on another blind raise?'

"Naw," laughed Woods. "I'd better look."

George began slipping his last draw card for a view. Four clubs he had now, four high ones with the joker, jack through ace, or ten through king. He needed a ten or ace of clubs to fill in his royal. Who was the teasing joker? Fat-boy? A lot of the gang thought of him as a joker, Port's personal court jester. A dim-witted clown, really. Well, if the clown wants to help, who am I to say no? The corner of his final card showed the top edge of a black ace! He made it, he made it! With a wide grin of triumph he tossed in fifty in chips.

"I'll just call you, Harg."

"Jesus, George," exhaled Wilkinson. "I got to see this!"

"So do I," disparaged Eskridge as he lay out his hand, a full house, red aces over three tens.

"My turn," replied George as he lay his cards face up one at a time and reciting each denomination. "King of clubs, queen of clubs, jack of clubs, and the joker for the ten"

"Looks like this was your hand after all," groaned Harg. "But let's see that last card, sport."

George turned it over with a smile of victory and flipped it atop his four exposed clubs. As he looked at it his smile froze and he blanched at the sight of the ace of spades. He had no flush, but a straight.

"George," grinned Eskridge, "this hand would be yours if you could turn that spade into a club. But as it is, my full house beats your straight."

As Harge raked in the chips Burt nodded in sympathy while George sat stunned, trying to understand how he could have misread his hand. What in the world was he seeing? In stony silence he was unable to comprehend the harsh betrayal his life was taking. It was a dark road. And rocky.

The life of an unhorsed knave was not a happy one.

FOURTEEN

Woods had no problem finding work in Durango as a part-time carpenter and laborer. Too, he found himself welcoming the time spent away from the gang, although he still palled about with a few close friends of the group. He also had joined them twice for forays into New Mexico to help gather cows and horse-flesh. But there was just something about Ike Stockton which made him uneasy, as if he were hiding behind a mask, untrustworthy-like. Ike's brother Port was exactly what he was, a short-tempered fuse with no hesitation to blow anybody's head off. But you knew where you stood with him, absolutely no subterfuge whatsoever, and you knew never to argue with him. If you believed he was wrong, or didn't agree with an opinion of his, you shut up or walked away, and that was that. George actually grew to like him once he was familiar with his ways. But of course if it weren't for his feelings towards Emily there was no way in the world he would have even thought of remaining in his company longer than it took him to mount his horse.

"Well, hell, ol' buddy," spoke Wilkinson one night with his usual infectious grin as he and Woods were hoisting beers at Elitch's Clam House in Durango. "I think you must be planning on hanging up your running-iron and six-gun, way you been keeping your nose to the grindstone of honest labor."

"More I work at legal peonage the more I'm getting to like it," returned Woods with a smile. "No insult intended, Bert, but I'm not cut out for renegading other people's wares. Get's me uneasy."

"Uneasy? Jesus. Them ranchers we take from started out in many cases as small thieves themselves that just growed more honest as their herds got bigger. Now they get testy when the tables are turned and the chickens come home to roost."

"True as dirt. And I still go out now and then with the boys south of the line when they need me, but mostly for the sweet scenery and to exercise my horse," he grinned. "Yet one day soon that'll stop too. I'll chuck it all away. Once you get caught it could be your last, like for instance being trussed up and ending up a decoration on a tree-limb."

"Shhhhit," poo-poohed Wilkinson. "Ain't a tree in the state got my name on it."

"Hope not, Bert. But that's one prediction no collector of another man's cows can describe."

"By the way, heard the latest?"

"Don't believe so. Ain't seen any of the gang in near a week."

"Well, listen to this. Ike is pissed at the Coe bunch for putting a two-thousand dollar bounty on his head. You know that, don't you?"

"Yeah. We all know that. And I sure wouldn't want to be in his boots or saddle."

"Well, Ike in revenge is getting thirty, forty of the gang together for a raid on Farmington."

"You got to be kidding."

"In a week, ten days, a bunch of us are going to gallop on down there and tear that town apart. It'll be another Lawrence, Kansas raid. Gonna make Bloody Bill Anderson look like a Sunday school teacher."

"Bert, Ike has to be out of his mind. He's smarter than that."

"Naw. He's just gonna beat 'em to the punch because of the bounty they put on him. He calls it a 'preemptive' strike, whatever that fancy word means."

"It means, hitting before you're hit."

"Yep. That's it."

"What really made him decide on such a half-witted idea?"

"Remember 'Kid' White? The lame-brained one-notch killer?"

"Yeah. A mental light-weight."

"The other night he made the mistake of trying to kill Ike."

"Good, god, you mean he was simple enough to try to draw on him?"

"No, nothing that stupid."

"So what'd he do, walk up to him and make a citizen's arrest?"

"Har, har, that's a good one, George!"

"Well, the suspense is killing me. Out with it."

"The Kid and Ike was out on a one-horse buggy going from bar to bar on a drinking spree after the Kid offered to treat him to an afternoon of barhopping. But Ike didn't know that the Kid was offered nine-hundred dollars to kill him, and wanted to get him drunk to shoot him. Mid-way in their toot one of the boys got the word and he hunted them down so as to warn Ike. After the man whispers the news in Ike's ear, he turns to the Kid with a big grin and asks, "What do you plan to do with the nine-hundred dollars, Kid?"

"That dumb Kid," sighed Woods. "Walked right into the lion's den."

"He turned white as a Kansas virgin and started stuttering and stammering a mile a minute, making absolutely no sense. Talking in tongues, they say. Finally Ike draws his Colt slow as molasses and points it between the Kid's eyes. The Kid stopped stuttering and stood wide-eyed and open-mouthed. Ike then says nonchalant-like, 'Go on and draw, Kid. Earn your keep.'"

"Then what happened?"

"The Kid can't say a word he's so froze up. Just stands there and watches as Ike lazily cocks his gun. The one notch at a time of the four clicks can be heard nice and clear a mile away. Four or five of the boys was there and they just watch like it was a play. Ike waits in charitable patience a few more seconds in case the Kid decides to draw, then out of kindness pulls the trigger. The Kid, still wide-eyed, but now with a blank stare, is sprawled on his back in the road like he was hit with a two by four."

"I bet nobody saw any brains leaking out the back of his head, neither."

"Nope. Nary a drop, partner. Nary a drop."

"You know, I do believe he was so dumb he had to have been kin to your old pal, Comanche Bill."

"He, hah, hah!" guffawed Bert. "You got that right!"

"I heard one time someone caught the Kid trying to load the cylinder of his six-shooter with the bullets backwards."

This brought an even greater roar of laughter from Bert, who was holding the bar with both hands in fear of falling.

"Not only that," Woods went on in a serious vein. "But in the Kid's pocket the undertaker found a long shopping list totaling nine-hundred dollars."

By now Bert was helpless and weak from riant laughter, with tears pouring down his face as he begged Woods to stop, half leaning on the bar to keep his feet. "Oh, god, George! Please, not another word! No More!"

Appearing before them behind the bar was the well-dressed and rotund proprietor, John Elitch. "You boys sound like you're having one hell of a good time. Nothing makes my heart gladder than to see my customers enjoying themselves!"

"Why, hello there, Big John," greeted Woods. "Yeah, we're having a great chuckle here."

"Well, have a pair of brandys on me, George, Bert," he replied, pouring a healthy amount of French cognac into a pair of large snifters. "Always pleases me to see you two gentlemen."

"Why, thank you, Big John. We'll certainly drink to that, right Bert?"

Wiping his face and eyes with his handkerchief, Bert nodded, "You bet. Thanks, John."

"You boys keep laughing now," smiled Elitch with a wave of his hand, exiting the bar for the floor crowded with dinner-feasting customers.

"Whew!" exhaled Bert. "This French pizon is the grandest firewater I ever did drink!"

"Yessiree," echoed Woods. "Could be habit-forming, if I could afford it."

"So anyway, George. You coming along?"

"Where?"

"On the Farmington raid. How about it?"

"No, I can't. I got a good job and don't want to lose it."

Wilkinson slowly shook his head back and forth, hardly believing what he was hearing. "We can sure use a gun like yours. Steady and true you are. And hell, we're all gonna wear hoods. Practically invisible is what we'll be. C'mon, George. Make it your last caper. Retire in style."

"Nope. Can't. Something tells me it's a fool's errand. I want to commit suicide, I'll do it by my own hand.

FIFTEEN

While Ike was gathering his army together, rumors, which traveled unbelievably swift between the two communities, were rife in Farmington of Stockton's planned strike. Wasting no time the Coes immediately set out with their own preemptive force of forty-some members with the ambitious and determined intent of capturing and arresting the entire Stockton-Eskridge clan.

The next night, on a balmy Sunday of 16 April a little past 11 p.m., the Coe group, led by rancher Cox, astride their mounts two and three abreast, unobtrusively entered the murky edge of Durango. It was quite dark, but they could see to their left across a wide field, silhouetted by windowed lights of some businesses along the far street, a great gathering. Dimly distinguishable clots of excited groups shifted and milled about like busy ants and chattering chipmunks up and down and back and forth, some bearing torches. There may have been several hundred or so, and before too long the Farmington Minutemen realized they had ridden plumb into the center of the old established ritual called, "rope justice." Someone was being lynched.

Earlier in the evening a drunken Stockton gang member, Henry Read Moorman, had given the Coliseum Theater of Durango another black eye by shooting to death James K. Prindle, a miner, and wounding Percy Stoffee. In moments a pair of lawmen overpowered the inebriated assailant and dragged him off to the slammer. It was a mystery why Moorman committed the senseless act in the first place for it seemed neither of the men knew him, nor he them. Alcoholic insanity, the more astute opined. Whatever the case, it wasn't long before an enraged citizenry of about 300 with opinions of their own made an appearance at the hoosgow at eleven o'clock. Breaking open the door they dragged the still-soused tenant out of the building, down the street, and attached him to one of the few trees which lined Main Avenue. They then jubilantly cheered as his protesting body kicked and squirmed its life away on the limb of a pine, and where it remained in undisturbed suspension until the next day.

The New Mexico vigilantes, being no stranger to the primitive judicial ceremony, paid their respects by silently continuing on to Animas City so as not to disturb nor delay the civil proceedings.

They had more important work to do anyway, and it would be careless indeed to reveal their intent at that precarious moment, possibly fatal. It would be like kicking an ant hill, an unkindness which would certainly not be appreciated. Let sleeping dogs lie.

After spending the night unobtrusively throughout the wooded countryside, they arose mid-morning ready for action. Nance and the Coes called on Sheriff Hunter and asked him to arrest the Stockton-Eskridge bunch, then hand them over. Unimpressed, the sheriff agreed to do so as soon as they presented him with the proper paperwork. Grumbling, they left to discuss their next move. Sometime during the night the town had been alerted that renegades were in the neighborhood, so armed men patrolled the streets. This of course spoiled for the raiders what surprise they may have had, so in the morning they mounted up and took to the high ground, namely a long mesa just east of town. As they walked their horses like tourists along the rim for a bird's view of the neighborhood, they were spotted by a few eager Minutemen who sent a few shots toward them.

"What's that?" puzzled Woods at the muffled sounds over his late breakfast of scrambled eggs and buffalo steak in a nearby café.

"I think them's shots, ol' buddy," answered Wilkinson, sliding back his chair for a casual walk to the door.

George rose up to join him. As they emerged on the boardwalk they heard scattered gunshots coming from on high and saw riders strung out on the distant mesa. A few rounds hit the dirt street before them, raising small clouds of dust. A ping or two echoed lazily in the sun as ricocheted rounds hit metal roofs.

"It's them damn New Mexico bandits!" shouted a young rifleman to George who was busy picking his teeth, trying to free a buffalo-shard. Pointing toward the mounted line he added, "They come all the way from Farmington!"

"Do tell," commented George. "Loan me your rifle a sec, will you son?"

The teenager wasn't sure he should when Wilkinson said, "Ain't you Fred Tyler's boy?"

"Yes, sir."

"Well, hell," retorted Bert. "It's okay, you can give it to him. I know your pa real well."

As the young man extended the Winchester, Bert said to George, "Seems that big-gutted turd up there on that mangy mount looks kinda familiar, you know?"

"Damn if it ain't. Appears to be Big Dan Howland."

"Bet you a beer you can't get him."

"Oh, c'mon, now. Piece of cake, Bert."

"Ain't for me, that's why I ask you to do it."

"How about two beers? One for him, and one for the nag?"

"Well now, you are a sporting man, ain't you?'

"Well, I'm kinda thirsty."

"All right, you're on."

The riders were sending more shots over the town, and the two men and boy moved back toward the building under the shade of the awning for better protection. George slid a round into the chamber and aimed toward the large man astride his mount. For George's convenience Big Dan stopped a moment to raise his own rifle to send off several shots town-ward, unknowingly making himself a perfect target. "Horse first, Bert," he announced, then squeezed the trigger. A second after his shot Big Dan's horse crumpled to the ground. Slamming another round into the chamber George had the rifle ready for Howland, but he had disappeared. "Damn! Why'd I do it all ass-backwards? I should have got him first. All I did was put a bucket of soap out of misery."

"True enough, but Dan's life saved me a beer. Too bad, though. He's a louse."

"Here's your gun, boy. Thank you."

"You're welcome, sir."

The two reentered the café to finish their breakfast as the failed raiders soon rode away toward New Mexico. They left behind the carcass of Howland's horse and two slightly wounded bystanders in town. Glancing bullets hit Conrad Polvurmiller in the leg, and Henry Wilson in the hand.

SIXTEEN

Several days following the blunted incursion from Farmington, the Durango *Record* blithely boasted that the town had a thousand armed men prepared to repel any invasion of their community. But it was a brag in poor taste, for they failed to consider the danger to innocent non-combatants. The toot sounded more like a sportscast and was unappreciated by a portion of fed-up citizens who now lost sympathy with their home-grown thugs. So they formed a Committee of Safety and immediately invited Ike Stockton, the Eskridge brothers, Jim Garrett, Jack Wilson and others to leave town. At this stern announcement the Eskridge brothers came unglued, and when town marshal Bob Dwyer attempted cooling them down, the pair drew and flaunted their six-shooters.

Next, as a demonstration of democracy in action, the pro-Stockton camp-followers immediately called a meeting of their own to express their feelings for the gang, labeling them good, law-abiding citizens who had defended the town from alien invaders, and vowed to protect them. But when the Stockton-Eskridge coterie heard of Farmington taking the step of legally filing indictments against them, a handful saw the writing on the wall and thought putting miles between them and Durango might not be a bad idea. Accepting a gift of $700 from sympathizers, a handful rode out. Yet to make the atmosphere a bit more binding for those who remained behind, when the Colorado cattlemen attempted to round up their free-grazing herds in New Mexico during the May roundup, they were informed by the Coe cartel that no Colorado stock would be allowed to leave New Mexico until Ike Stockton was arrested and handed over to them. While Colorado herdsmen fumed over this knotty problem, with a few no doubt toying with the idea of casting Ike to the wolves, fate stunningly appeared with a temporary surcease for Ike. And of all things, it came in the form of a small Indian uprising.

Approximately 200 miles northwestward, in the bordering territory of Utah, white settlers and Native Utes and Piutes were on the warpath with each other. It had been building for a year, and it concerned the old story of manifesting Anglos encroaching on the Native's constantly shrinking lands. Finally some blood was shed on 1 May 1881, when three men were attacked by a roving band of Natives, two of them left dead. One of the men was from Colorado, just across the line, and his body was brought back for burial by his two brothers, George and Billy May. With them at the discovery of Dick May's corpse was ex-Cimarronite Henry C. Goodman, now a rancher.

The small band connected with additional members and continued riding south, stealing whatever horses or anything of value they came across. In time numbering about forty, and with perhaps sixty women, children, elders, a herd of goats and an accumulation of perhaps 350 filched equine, they u-turned north. They were making toward the La Sal Mountains, roughly 120 miles distant, a march across a stretch of desert to the forested high ground. Word of course spread, and in the interim five posses formed which took to the field, three from Colorado and two from Utah.

It was a rabid Billy May who rode into Rico on 28 May to loudly sound the alarm of his brother's murder which gave birth to the first posse. This also was when the clever and calculating Ike Stockton saw and grasped the opportunity of recouping his now somewhat tarnished reputation, by voluntarily joining them in recapturing their stolen stock. All the volunteers moved west 35 miles to Big Bend to finally organize, then rode off into the wild and rugged country of Utah to give the Redmen their due, with leader William Dawson in charge of the fifty-man posse. Among them were Stockton and his lieutenant Harg Eskridge, and cronies Marion Cook and "Kid" Roberts.

The men rode, tracked and climbed throughout the sun-burning desert, hills and arroyos and creeks, intensely scouting, some to reclaim lost stock, others for the sport of the kill. The wearisome trek dragged on for a little over two weeks. Since most of the men were unfamiliar with the endlessly rough terrain, the Natives held the advantage and knew it. Too, some of Dawson's men would break up into small search parties of their own, while now and then a few too tired to go on would return to Colorado. Neither was it an ideal, cohesive company, with bickering, ego-plays and general dissatisfaction reeking the atmosphere. By 9 June they were down to thirty-three men.

On 15 June they had been steadily climbing upward along the side of a wooded mountain in the La Sal Range amid the rocky and arroyo-slashed country of Pinhook Draw, now afoot and reduced to eighteen men. They were approaching the area which would become the bloody confrontation between the two groups. Knowing the foe was near, but practically invisible due to the forest and the high, dense, brush, which was difficult to make their way through, Dawson sent eight men forward to scout and ascertain the location of the enemy. Within a short time the advance party was ambushed and trapped. Pinned down by a furious cross fire from the high ground, most were killed or wounded. Hell then broke loose and shooting then became general with a secluded enemy. This was when Harg Eskridge took a bullet. Now left with ten men, Dawson wondered at his fate.

That evening to his small relief he was joined by perhaps a dozen men who were a part of the group left behind with the horses. The following morning another dozen or so members of the Maob posse also joined them. About noon, Dawson, realizing his critical predicament, although thankful for the small reinforcements, sent D.G. Taylor to ride like the devil back to Rico for help. Another man, Tom Pepper, also wished to go, but Dawson refused him, needing what manpower they had. Yet, to Dawson's anger and frustration, Pepper instantly and ardently mounted his horse and glued himself to the galloping Taylor like a latter-day Revere with not even courteous goodbye.

Around two in the afternoon the firing appeared to have melted away from the high grounded defenders, who had slowly departed to leave the battle ground to the near-exhausted Anglos. By four, Dawson accepted the silence as a sign they had withdrawn, so did so himself. The serious part of the campaign was now ended, with neither side victors in the thankless fight, although some stock was recovered. The final toll was eight Anglos and twenty-two Natives dead. There were some who sustained serious wounds, such as Harg Eskridge, having his heel shot off.

With help from the Moab posse, the wounded were mounted or wagoned, depending on the seriousness of their infirmities, and down the mountain they proceeded. Their destination was west to Moab, perhaps fifteen miles.

It was at 4 a.m. the next morning when the party reached the edge of Moab, and at the Peter Rasmussen ranch the wounded were examined and cared for. Harg was in a deep fever, and his foot wound looked so rancid and was so badly discolored, some men strongly suggested amputation to save his life. But Stockton just as strongly suggested they had better wait—or else. Not caring to cross the man, they silently agreed. It was Rasmussen's daughter Margaret, having nursing experience, who tended Eskridge's shattered heel with a poultice and miraculously saved his foot.

The fifth and last group to head into Utah was also from Rico, and called the "Rescue Posse." D.G. Taylor, the rider dispatched by Dawson, arrived there on 21 June to breathlessly describe the posse's plight, so it was quickly organized with the idea of rescuing the men from a dire situation. Dyson Eskridge, learning of his brother's wound, plus Gus Hefferman and Bert Wilkinson, were among them, as also none other than the owner, publisher and editor of the Rico *Dolores News,* and Ike Stockton's public relations champion, Charles Adam Jones. On the edge of the dusty street filled with busy men moving about was George Woods and Bert Wilkinson.

"Hey, George," called Burt in excitement to his companion standing amused on the boarded walk, calmly observing the goings on. Bert had slid his Winchester into its saddle-sheath for perhaps the tenth time, after checking and rechecking it, making sure it was loaded, so charged up he was. "Why don't you come along? This is gonna be some lark, let me tell you. Might even collect a scalp or two!"

"Naw, not me, Bert. I'm not one to volunteer for a hot, miserable ride chasing ghosts. Those Utes will ride circles around you, knowing the country as they most likely do."

"But, damn, we can sure use a gun handler such as you."

"No, thanks, ol' buddy. I ain't got nothing against them Redskins. They never done me no wrong. But bring me back a pair of moccasins if you have a mind to. Autographed by Geronimo would be nice."

"Well, if I come across him in my sights, I surely will," he laughed.

The next day they eagerly rode off on their mission of mercy, not realizing the battle was over near a week. Dyson and Hefferman traveled with the rescue party to the La Sal Mountains and the scene of the battle site, but before long broke off from them and returned to Rico, rejoined once again with Ike, Marion and the wounded Harg.

The gang members of the crusading effort found to their joy they were now looked upon as conquering heros by the local citizenry. When the *Conejos County Times* dared dispute the accolades and cast disparagement upon the ex-combatants, Jones of the *Dolores News* stood up and defended them in editorial anger. But the crusaders' place in the sun would be a brief aura for them, with a series of disastrous circumstances which would terminate in black and tragic overtones.

SEVENTEEN

It all began innocuously enough on a mild August afternoon with four cowboys casually riding and drinking from bar to bar; George Woods, Bert Wilkinson, Jim Catren and "Black Kid" Thomas. They were actually on a journey to pick up the stashed loot from a stagecoach robbery of a few weeks before. Thomas' older brother had a lucky day hitting the stage alone, knowing they were carrying a small payroll with only the driver and one man riding shotgun. After racing off with the loot he was unaware that a pair of ranchers just beyond the hill behind the coach came riding up and were informed of the deed. The shotgun rider knew who the culprit was, even though he was wearing a bandana over his face, and so informed the ranchers who immediately galloped to town with the news. That night Black Kid's brother described to him where he had hidden the money for a later retrieval, but unfortunately was caught the next day and strung up. Black Kid waited a few weeks, then quit his construction job, picking up two week's pay. He should have dug up the payroll and quietly left town, but on his way to the cache site he stopped in a saloon to have a beer.

Meeting a trio of cowboys whom he knew he bought them a round of beers, then a second, then a third, feeling magnanimous with his last wages, and before long let them in on his secret. The three were only too glad to join Thomas on his odyssey of retrieval, then had a fourth round. On the way they stopped several more times, and before long Thomas was broke. So Jim Catren, in his loose state of mind, suggested they rob someone.

"You can't be serious, Jim," commented George.

"Hell, yes," emphasized Catren, not focusing too well.

"Sure," echoed Bert with a laugh, with Thomas heartily agreeing also. "Let's call it 'investing in our future'."

"Well, fellows, I'm all for digging up someone else's loot, and even collecting stray cows and horses now and then. And I'll even shoot a man off his horse who appears to be shooting at me, even though I did mistakenly nail Big Dan's horse instead of him, damn it. But when it comes to outright holdups, count me out."

"Aw, George," admonished Bert. "Nothing to it. And we don't aim to kill, only rob."

"Naw, robbery ain't in my makeup. Really. You fellows go on without me. I've had too much to drink anyway, and I'd better head for the barn afore I get in somebody's gunsights."

Catren looked upon George demeaningly and said, "Ah, hell, go on home then. We sure as hell don't need anyone to hold our horses. One less to split with anyway."

To their honking laughter George shook his head at their foolishness and rode off.

The trio then cantered down the road, pulled up at an isolated saloon, robbed it, and galloped on, laughing and guffawing at nothing in particular except the fun they were having.

Soon they were in Durango where they had more beer, and Catren was arrested for insulting a deputy. But soon they freed their companion and fled, continuing on their destination. On the way out of town without Catren they were joined by Dyson Eskridge, and together the three cantered toward Silverton.

The men were spotted by mine owner and stableman Emerson W. Hodges who was also horsing to Silverton. Knowing the men were wanted by the law, upon his arrival he notified town Marshal Claton Ogsbury and San Juan County Sheriff George Thorniley of their future guests. Arriving a bit later, the three desperados left their horses at Hodges' stable next to Bronco Lou's "Diamond Saloon," a combination bar, dance hall and whore house, and entered for a little R&R. Although it was known by then the trio were wanted men, the sheriff had no warrants. So the law patiently decided to retire for the night and check the morning's stage for warrants on them.

A little after eleven that night La Plata County Sheriff Luke Hunter arrived in Silverton with warrants for the fugitives. Luke was a close crony of the Stocktons, and probably a silent partner, in that he took

Port's place as the gang's protector-about-town. Some thought his task that night was to apprehend the three waywards, return them to Durango, then release them on a light bond. Whatever the case, Hunter seemed to nonchalantly kill time by socializing and gabbing with many of the men who were about the streets at that hour, instead of immediately contacting the law.

Coming across mine owner Hodges, Hunter proceeded with him to the Senate Saloon where Marshal Ogsbury was sleeping in a back room. At the bar was Dick Simms, and after hearing enough of the conversation between Hunter, Hodges, and the proprietor John Goode, Simms swiftly slunk off to warm the three celebrants at Bronco Lou's. As Ogsbury dressed he suggested they round up a few more men, like maybe the sheriff, to be on the safe side, since the men would be armed with booze and bullets both.

"Aw, no problem, Marshal," downplayed Hunter. "I know all three and they won't give us any trouble at all."

Ogsbury and Hodges exchanged doubtful glances a moment, then acquiesced.

"Well, o. k., Hunter," replied Ogsbury. "Let's go."

The three men, a pair of armed marshals and an unarmed civilian, proceeded to the Diamond Saloon two blocks away. Passing the livery stable where the outlaws left their horses and rifles, they approached the dance hall next door on the street corner. Raucous music could be heard mingled with drunken laughter. In the lead and walking up to the saloon to his left, Ogsbury saw an individual in the shadows by the door. Moving toward the man cautiously, the Marshal reflected just enough light on his upper body to reveal who he was, badge and all. As he was about to address the dark figure a gunshot exploded with a flash of light and Ogsbury was hit just below the heart, felling him to the ground. As Hodges bent and turned the Marshal over, hoping to be able to help, a staccato of shots suddenly rang out which caused him to run for cover. After the shooting Hodges returned to the Marshal's prone body to hear his last moan. Hunter was nowhere in the vicinity. Hodges entered the saloon for help, and two men returned with him outside to help carry the lawman's corpse back to Goode's Saloon. As they were proceeding with the deceased between Bronco Lou's and the stable, the three desperados ran in panic from Bronco Lou's and off to the outskirts of town, leaving their horses and rifles behind at the stable.

A handful of citizens, alerted as to what happened, rode in all directions seeking the trail of the horseless killers. The fire bell was rung and phone calls were made to several outlaying towns to sound the alarm. It was soon found they fled westward, and with torches it could be seen where they blindly sloshed through knee-deep mud for a time in the darkness.

Roughly an hour later Black Kid Thomas surrendered, saying he had nothing to do with the killing. Whatever the truth, it was thought his mission was to return to the stable for the horses and rifles, a thankless assignment at best, for they had been confiscated knowing to whom they belonged. To tighten up loose ends, that afternoon the Kid was taken from his cell and hanged for being in bad company. What soured his pleas of innocence were several witnesses in the dance hall who said he had fired at least four of the shots. Later it was found he was not the killer of the marshal, plus also the city had lost a bit of investment, for the Kid had a $1,200 Texas reward on him.

Marshall Hunter too was taken to task and later horse-whipped in the papers for his lackadaisical performance in the affray, especially for not coming to the aid of a fellow officer in peril, and merely disappearing. The editorial questioned whether Hunter was a member of the gang; was he an accessory; was Simms too a go-between? Also, while Hunter rode the forty-seven miles from Durango horseback, he quickly returned in comfort via stage, and Simms gladly did him the favor of riding his horse to Durango to escape the heat. Hunter too may have realized it would be foolish for him to linger any longer in Silverton with these fiery tempers roasting the atmosphere.

Eskridge and Wilkerson, in their flight westward, and staying off whatever main trails there were, naturally thought of Rico as a place of refuge. But spotting Sheriff Thorniley and his posse the next day from afar put a damper on that idea. So they decided to make their way to the Castle Rock station where friends Orville and Flora Pyle and Simeon and Ellen Hendrickson fed them, then agreed to stock them with whatever provisions they needed while in hiding. They also provided them with a pair of horses. Too, a miner headed toward Animas City carried word from the two bravos to Harg where they were secreted. Meanwhile in Silverton the reward for the shooter of the marshal, now accepted as Wilkinson, topped off at $2,500. Also, stalwart editor Charles Jones of the Rico *Dolores News,* who yet remained one of the last of the Stockton-Eskridge cheering section, spent some time traipsing the mountains with a burro seeking the two members at large. He even had provisions for them. When he accidently bumped into Thorniley's posse in the wild, he tactfully said nothing of his mission, or compassionate intent.

In Animas City Harg passed on the miner's information to Ike, who immediately went to Marshal Hunter asking that he and Cook be deputized to bring in the two men. Hunter, desiring to distance himself as far as possible from the growing Wilkinson quicksand pit, happily complied. The pair then loaded up with supplies and set out on horseback for Castle Rock.

Ike couldn't have asked for a more qualified individual as a fit crony. Marion Cook was actually Marion "Bud" Galbreath, wanted in Bosque County, Texas for rape and the murder of a deputy sheriff back when only seventeen. Now twenty-four, he was a seasoned fugitive who also claimed on his resume the brief honor of being a one-time member of John Wesley Hardin's clan.

As the pair rode to the rescue of the waiting renegades, Ike revealed his scheme to his very willing cohort. Once finding the two they would work out a story to separate Dyson from Bert. It was Bert Ike wanted, and naturally for the reward. He believed by fattening his wallet he would also be looked upon with appreciation as a concerned citizen bringing in the cold-blooded killer of the law. The social elevation fed his calculating imagination. But he had to get Dyson out of the picture, for he knew Harg would be out to kill him in a split second if he dared arrest his brother. It was not so much that Ike feared him, but he desired to avoid messy complications. Cook also looked forward to the termination of the scheme in which they would split the reward, $1,250 each.

Ike Stockton knew the Pyles and Hendricksons of Castle Rock, yet when they rode up were greeted a bit frostily. The concealers of the two gang members were always chary of Ike, and now more cautious with a stranger at his side, not knowing Cook-Galbreath.

"Howdy, Simeon," hailed Ike with his best toothy smile. "Orville," he nodded.

"Well, hello, Ike," greeted Orville with a weak grin. "Been a long time."

"That's for certain, Orville. Hope all is well with you people here."

"Well as could be, Ike," replied Orville. Simeon stood back to let Orville have the stage, feeling more secure in a muted state.

Ike jumped right in. "Guess you done heard of Bert and Dyson? Their trouble up in Silverton?"

"Yeah, some of it. Awful, too. Can hardly believe it."

"I know, Orville. It was Kid Thomas done the marshal. And to prove it, they drug him right out of his cell and lynched him. Now they're after Bert and Dison to even the score."

"Don't see how that's justice, seeing as the Kid done it."

"Me neither, that's for sure. So we come to get them two boys out of here and down to Mexico, pronto, to save their necks."

Orville stood silent, confused, wondering which way to turn, smelling trouble, wanting to protect his friend Wilkinson, thinking he should say nothing. "Ain't that lawman's badges you boys are wearing?"

Ike wanted to kick himself. "Uh," he stumbled. "Oh, hell, we ain't the law, Orville. We just went to Hunter and had him give us these tin stars to wear so we could move around easier, in case someone saw us, you know? To hurry and get them out of here, quick and safe."

Cook sat his horse, impatient, restless, wondering what in hell was wrong with Ike, wanting to use a little persuasion. He felt these yokels knew where the two were hiding and were just killing time. Damn them.

"Orville?" spoke his wife of a sudden behind him, hearing the talk. "Oh, is that you, Ike?"

She smiled warmly.

"Sure is, Flora," answered Stockton lightly. "And how you be?"

"Just fit and fine, Ike. So good to see you."

Flora was always taken by Ike and his gentlemanly manners and attention, even though her husband was more critical.

"We just dropped by, Flora, to help Bert and Dyson out of the country. And we really have to hurry."

"Ohhh," she went on, "ain't it awful? And getting the blame, too!"

"Yessiree, it is," he echoed. "Plain tragic."

Orville wanted to say something to stop his wife from saying any more, but it was too late.

"Well," she continued, in a waterfall of words. "We done fed them and hid them out back in the woods. I'm sure they'll be glad to see you, Ike! And I'm so glad you are here to help get them out of all that trouble!"

Orville gave up and added, "They're a mile or so back in them thick clump of trees. In a small clearing. Just go straight along that small arroyo there, about a quarter mile, then veer to the right behind those woods."

"Much obliged, Orville, Flora. We got to get going now, folks. Thank you again," and the pair trotted off. Once out of talking distance Ike spoke quickly, "Best we put these badges in our pockets, old buddy. Afore we blow the whole works!"

They made the described turn and walked their mounts slowly and carefully through the trees. Shortly, they came across the trail-worn and scruffy Eskridge and Wilkinson bent over a low fire. Ike greeted jocosely, "I hope that coffee's drinkable, boys!"

In a start the two fugitives jumped and turned, half-reaching for their sidearms.

"Whoa, settle down!" laughed Ike, both hands upraised. "Be a little more friendly to your rescuers. We come to free Caesar, not bury him!"

"Damn it, Ike, Marion," exclaimed Dyson. "You done scared the holy shit out of us! Sure good to see you both, though!"

"That goes double," echoed Bert. "I'm sure sick of this mountain picnicking."

"Well, all that's over for you now. You two are going on to Old Mexico for awhile til things cool down. Me and Marion will escort you part way."

Ike then went into a brief but convincing plan for the two which Eskridge and Wilkinson gladly went along with. "Now, first thing we got to do is get a fresh pair of horses for you. Them nags'll never get you off this mountain. Dyson, I want you to ride on out to Morrison's ranch in the valley and get a pair of strong and stout mounts for the trip. You go on now, and we'll wait here for you. Now git, and don't waste any time."

Not fives minutes after Dyson hurriedly trotted away, Ike reached over and pulled Bert's six-gun from his holster.

"What you doing, Ike?" a puzzled Wilkinson inquired.

"You won't be needing this, Bert," Ike retorted, after which he snapped on a pair of cuffs on the stunned prisoner. "Now climb aboard that nag of yours and let's move."

EIGHTEEN

As soon as Ike Stockton and Marion Cook returned with Wilkinson to Animas City, they hid him the first night in the timbered hills behind town, not taking a chance on losing their investment to a lynch mob. The next morning Ike informed Luke Hunter of their capture, then made the necessary contacts with Silverton authorities for arrangements for the pay-off. He next put Bert up at Jeff Keith's Cattleman Hotel east of town across the Animas River, then allowed a reporter a brief interview of the prisoner so as to remove any doubt of his apprehension, especially to the Silverton crowd.

Bert presented to the scribe quite a ragged sight, wearing the same clothes as the night of the shooting hardly a week before. A cartridge belt circled his waist, and the soles of his bare feet showed through the bottom of his worn boots. Tattered and scruffy as he appeared, he sat back during the exchange casually smoking a Meerschaum pipe. His main concern seemed about getting a fair trial, after which the newsman inquired if he had any statement to make as to the Silverton incident. "They are for strangling," came his depressed and unvarnished reply, the Black Kid's swift demise leaning heavily on his mind. He labeled the Kid's lynching a foul murder, seemingly forgetful of the marshal's foul murder which set the distressful episode off in the first place.

George Woods had been in Bill Valliant's Saloon in Animas City nearly an hour chain-drinking beer in an unexplainable funk. He was in the grip of a strange inner gnawing which kept growing the past day or two, and couldn't shake it, or throw it off. Something ugly was in the wind, and it sent a sudden chill down his spine. He wanted to have no part of it, whatever it was. It left an unsavory taste in his mind of an ominous foreboding.

It had been over an hour since he had talked briefly to his sometime-companion Wilkinson at Keith's Hotel. Ike was still busily in the process of contacting the Silverton authorities to make arrangements for an exchange: Bert for $2,500. Although Woods could see the writing on the wall as to Bert's future for the killing, it irked him to hear and see Ike bargaining so non-concernedly, as if Bert was little more than a lost cow Ike was returning to its owner for a finder's fee. Woods, standing at the bar unmindful of several of the gang raucously toasting the capture, turned and asked Ike if he could visit Bert briefly. Ike eyed him icily, pondering a moment, knowing he and Bert were occasional boozing buddies, and wondered in fleeting suspicion if George was going to try something.

"O.k., George. I'll walk you on over. But leave your gun here at the bar. Mind doing that?"

"No, fine with me." He parted his jacket and pulled his revolver from his waistband, adding in slight unhidden disgust, "I only want a visit. I got no mind to kill no one."

Ike gave a mean wince at the unexpected reply, for it was so unlike Woods. Although a good man with a gun he was mostly a quiet one, satisfied to remain in the background, making no waves or threats. Woods in turn caught the deadly flash in Ike's eyes, and in turn wished he'd been less glib. Especially with Ike, who like Port, wouldn't hesitate shooting a man, armed or not, back or front. He also did not realize until too late that his comment in Stockton's mind could be taken as a challenge. The beer made him careless. Hoping to make a symbolic show of pacification, Woods handed his Colt to Bill Valliant saying, "I'll be back to reclaim this shortly," and left the bar with Ike behind him.

It was a dark and moonless night, and since George knew by now where Bert was being kept, he walked east toward the bridge that crossed the Animas. Ike offered no conversation, only guardedly trailing behind and slightly to the right, more a sentinel than a companion. On the bridge over the dark rippling water George grew a bit nervous, so thought a word or two might soften the growing tension he felt emanating from his mute trailer.

"How's Bert holding up?" ventured Woods over his shoulder, light as he could.

"Just fine, George, just peachy," came his gelid reply. "A little ragged from wear and tear, but still worth twenty-five hundred beautiful dollars."

George was repulsed at his cynical retort. How in hell could Stockton do this, turn in one of his own for the reward? True, Bert wasn't the brightest lantern in town, and it seems he did kill the marshal. But by the same token, for Ike to play the moral avenger was already causing an undertow of disgust throughout Animas City. Didn't he realize he had crossed the line, and that his gesture was no more admirable than a Judas-act? People were funny that way, equating Bert's killing the marshal to Ike's riding a tainted white horse. No Lancelot there, that's for sure. So George gave up his attempt at conversation fearing he might make matters worse. Plus, he was unarmed.

The two continued their trek in silence, crossing the bridge and walking in the middle of the dirt street. To their right was the long frame building of Phil Garron's Room & Board house. Next, came the cabins of Pruett and Fowler. Then Keith's hotel, also on their right. Woods opened the door and entered, holding it agape for Stockton.

"That way," spoke Ike, as he placed his hand in the small of George's back to urge him forward, and to keep behind him. "Down the hall, second door."

As George opened the door and entered, he saw Bert sitting on the edge of the bed smoking his pipe. A pair of armed men sat in chairs, legs stretched out and crossed at the ankles, smoking cigarettes, Marion Cook and Jack Wilson. They looked at Woods hard-eyed, as if he were an unwelcome intruder and they had no use for him. They noted he was unarmed.

"Where's your pistola, Georgie?" came Cook's sarcastic comment. "You a boy scout now?"

George ignored him and looked to Wilkinson as the latter rose from the bed and smiled.

"Damn, George!" he hailed. "Good to see a friendly face for a change!"

"Jesus, Bert, you look like hell," replied Woods with a frown, extending his hand for a grip. But Bert ignored it and instead gave him an over-enthusiastic abrazo, desperately needing friendly human contact.

"Sure good to see you, George, really!"

Trying to keep things light, Woods commented, "Least you could have done is bathed and shaved for this momentous occasion."

"Well, hell, old buddy," returned Bert with a self-conscious grin. "I couldn't find the soap!"

It suddenly struck Woods that Wilkinson was kept purposely in a slovenly state by Ike. He presented a more convincing portrait of a lawman-killer this way. Of what value to the imagination would a squeaky-clean desperado be? Woods knew also that he was standing on thin ice, and had better mind his words and manners. Stockton was edgy, Cook was itching for a notch, and who the hell knows what was going through Wilson's head? They were nasty people with nasty intentions, that was obvious. So he continued his visit with safe small talk the three guardsmen would have nothing to complain about. Too, he had to get out of here, and soon. He could feel the room pressing in on him over the pale words he and Bert exchanged. He could do no good here: Bert was now in the hands of his self-ordained fate. But one thing kept echoing in his brain over and over, that he had the good sense not to have joined the trio in their initial robbery which started all this mess.

George thankfully left the helpless feeling Wilkinson and returned to Valliant's in great need of liquid medicine. The place was thankfully quiet, the celebrants of justice having moved down the street to Dolph's Saloon. Three men sat at a corner table playing poker. Woods stood at end of the bar and ordered a beer.

Bill Valliant slid a filled mug and his Colt before him. "How's Bert doing?"

"Nervous as a Thanksgiving turkey," replied Woods as he slid his firearm behind his belt. "And can't blame him."

"Well, since he pulled the trigger, he's assigned the price." Then added in distaste, "Although I don't approve with the collector's method."

Both men over time had become close confidants, and shared opinions privately exchanged.

"Yeah, for sure. I'd rather see Bert go down shooting than delivered like a side of beef."

"There's a quiet uproar building over Ike's playing the solid citizen, if you know what I mean."

"The role's a bit rank, I'd say."

"I don't know what in hell's gotten into Ike. I know he can be as mean as any reptile crawling, but this time he's walked the plank and doesn't seem to know it."

"Well, they're taking Bert back into the hills again tomorrow. Animas City and Durango both seem to have an itch to string him up, and Ike wants to protect his future income. He's been bargaining back and forth with the Silverton people, wanting them to come down with the reward money for the exchange. He's nervous some bunch will jump them along the way, maybe even Bert's buddy Dyson."

"Sounds like he's got a tiger by the tail," grinned Valliant, "with all that jockeying for position."

And that is the way it went. After a day hidden in the wooded hill country Wilkinson was brought down under extra heavy guard, which included Mayor E. E. Fox, for an evening meeting with his sister, mother and step-father. His parents despairingly pleaded with town officials present to see that their son got a fair trial. Bert was then hustled back into hiding while arrangements continued, Ike wanting to eliminate any risk of losing Wilkinson. He strongly insisted Silverton's people come down with the money in exchange for Wilkinson; they wanted Ike to deliver his captive to Silverton for the reward. Ike earlier felt he had the hammer, but it was Silverton who held the monied mallet. Since they smelled Stockton's avaricious ploy disguised as a defender of justice, they stuck to their guns. Ike began to feel things were unraveling, that a loss of controlling the situation was slipping from him. His prisoner was becoming an albatross.

Following more tortuous haggling, Ike finally threw in the towel. San Juan County Sheriff George Thorniley and his deputy rode with the Stockton group from Animas City to the Levi Carson ranch. There, Thorniley sent his deputy on to Silverton to notify and bring down the waiting dozen-man posse to meet them further on, at Ten Mile.

At Ten Mile the two groups met. Stockton, as legal deputy for La Plata County, with his assistants Cook, Fox and Henry Hull, and the trussed-up Wilkinson, horsed together with Thorniley's posse northward, the seventeen men reaching Silverton at six p.m. There was a large crowd massed about the San Juan County Bank where Ike formally surrendered his millstone to Thorniley. Someone in the crowd had the boldness to inquire about the other wanted shooter, Dyson Eskridge. Ike and Marion replied stonily they hadn't seen him or knew where he was.

The officials then escorted an armed-to-the-teeth Stockton through the side door of the bank for the brief ceremony of delivering the reward. San Juan County had put up $1,500; Silverton $1,000. But since desperado Dyson Eskridge's presence was lacking in the great bargain of exchange, the reward delivered was not for the full $2,500. Still, Ike received $1,421.43 in Government scrip. He then left with his company of three to spend a somewhat uneasy night at the Walker House.

Yet now, after all the stress of higgling and negotiations, Stockton somehow felt robbed of any sense of achievement, or that he had anything worth celebrating. Ashes in his mouth, it was. The Silverton crowd oozed with undisguised loathing for what he had done and he was not inoculated against the reeking atmosphere. They did not look upon him as a lawman performing his righteous duty. He was a gluttonous headhunter turning in one of his own men for money. Period. Although they were elated to have Bert in their grasp, many would have loved to have locked Ike in the same cell with him. Stockton had sought social elevation, acceptance and congratulations for the deed, especially on top of his joining the Injun-hunting posse in Utah, tracking down the Red threat. But instead of increasing his stature in the community, his latest actions had turned him into a pariah. In great relief at 7:30 next morning, Sunday, he left with Cook for Animas City.

On the other hand, Wilkinson was left feeling less anxiety-ridden than gang leader/man hunter Stockton. Incarcerated in a log jail and well-guarded, he was somewhat surprised to awake alive and well Sunday morning, for he had resigned himself to a lynching. It was a quiet if not somewhat busy day of several interviews and a visit from his old friends and earlier refuge-givers, Orville and Flora Pyle. His mother had gotten sick over his plight and couldn't be brought to see him. The Pyles attempted to elicit a promise from the lawmen that Bert would get a fair trial. Discouraged at the displayed lack of enthusiasm, the couple soon departed. A photographer turned up and took a portrait of the prisoner as he prattled nonchalantly and smoked a cigar. Wilkinson finally admitted he had been shooting and trying to kill someone else that night, namely Luke Hunter. He explained he did not know Marshal Ogsbury, and since he and Dyson were shooting together in his direction how could anyone tell who was responsible for killing the lawman? And although Dyson now was running about free as a bird, he held no resentment toward him. It was Ike Stockton he would like to be alone with for just a few minutes, so he could kill him and give the law a good reason for executing him. He would be glad to be hanged for that, and die singing.

With these grey thoughts on this grey Sunday of intermittent drizzles Bert lolled about in his cell with nothing more to do but wonder what Monday would bring. Near ten that night his contemplative musings were interrupted by a group of masked men who "stormed" the hoosegow and "overwhelmed" the guards. They strung a rope across a roof beam within the jail, attached the noose around his neck, then stood him on a chair. Someone asked if he had anything to say.

"Nothing, gentlemen," Wilkinson replied gamely. "Adios!" he farewelled as he kicked away the chair.

NINETEEN

George Woods heard of Wilkinson's last night on earth near noon the following day, Monday, when he dropped in for lunch at Valliant's.

"You heard yet?" queried the proprietor.

"What's that?"

"Bert got stretched in Silverton last night."

"Ah, Christ. Damn vigilantes, I bet."

"You done won a free beer," replied Bill as he tapped one. "And here it is."

"Was it Stanley again?"

"Yes it was, and you win again. Damn, George, at this rate you'll put me out of business."

Pat Stanley was a fifty-year-old Silverton brick mason, and a gruff and tough veteran of the Mexican War and guerilla fighting in Nicaragua. It appears he took it upon himself to assiduously dole out hemp justice as if it were his new profession, in competition with his bricklaying trade. He had been the man behind the Black Kid Thomas party prior to Wilkinson's gala. Before them Henry Moorman and two others had taken the fall in honor of his dark avocation. Five known thus far.

"No surprise there," groused Woods. "We must be using the wrong weapons. He's got more notches on his rope than we both do with our irons."

"That's for damn certain," chuckled Valliant.

"Did Ike get his bag of silver from Silverton?"

"Not the full twenty-five hundred, since he shorted them on delivering Dyson. But he did come away with around fourteen-hundred."

"Hell, you know he had to let Dyson run free. Otherwise brother Harg would have trailed him all the way to hell for his scalp."

"True enough."

Woods took a long pull at his glass half-emptying it. Valliant poured his second winning beer and slid it before him commenting, "Must be a thirsty day."

"Surely is. And a hungry one. I'd better eat."

Since the cook was off to the grocery with a small shopping list, and they were the only inhabitants of the saloon, Valliant whipped up a beef sandwich and bowls of buffalo stew for them both. He then drew himself a beer and joined Woods at a corner table.

"Guess you know about Isaac Lacy?" inquired the barman.

"About his being killed over in Fort Lewis?"

"Yeah. Back-shot several times by Big Dan Howland."

"Howland," snorted Woods disgustedly. "How I do regret shooting his horse, guilty of nothing more than hauling around a sack of shit."

Valliant laughed. "Well put, George. I can't but wholeheartedly agree."

"Lacy was a tough but good man. He was only a bad judge of character."

"How's that?"

"The Stockton brothers were kin to his wife."

"Hell, you say? I didn't know that."

"Cousins of some sort. Sadly, Lacy held to the flawed belief that kin were a trustworthy lot."

"A deformity of thought if there ever was one."

"So Lacy foolishly hired Ike to be his range foreman for a time. That was like giving a starving wolf the key to the butcher shop. Lacy's partner George Thompson even warned him Ike was stealing his cows. To top it off, Lacy's partner at their Fort Lewis slaughtering house where they had the army beef contract, John Freeland, was running stolen cattle through it regularly, including Lacy's. I still squirm over that, for I helped shuttle some of them cows."

"Well, then, do you think Ike had anything to do with Lacy's shooting?"

"No, not really. Not that he'd of cared. He might of seen it coming, but naturally kept mum about it. I think It was the New Mexico bunch set him up for the kill."

"Rank bunch of people down there."

"Rank ones up here, too."

"You know, George, and I'm sure you suspected. The night Ike took you over to visit Bert at the hotel, he was looking to bury you."

"Yeah, I could sense it, and I was pretty nervous on the trip there, being unarmed with him walking a bit behind me. For one thing, he knows I've fallen out of being one of his cow collectors, having refused him the honor of my talent a couple times now. Told him I've retired."

"Smart move, George. But keep your distance from him."

"That I plan to do. Might even move up to Silverton awhile."

"Talk about leaving town, seems one of the Coes done pulled out for Lincoln awhile ago."

"Who's that?"

"George and his wife Phoebe with their child."

"Guess he got tired of dodging bullets."

"Seems like he come close to collecting a few. Tom Nance and a couple of his friends dropped in one night at the hotel in Durango they were staying at, looking to end his stay permanent-like. While they were at the downstairs bar someone went up and quick-like warned Phoebe. She then passed the news to George who knew he had to get out in a hurry. Knowing she was safe but were out to get him, he told his wife to stay, that he'd be back the next day with a wagon for her and the baby. Out the back window he went. Gutsy Phoebe meanwhile goes downstairs and confronts Nance and his companions, asking what they wanted. Tom smoothly tells her they were there to protect her husband, hearing some men were in town to do him harm. She says they don't need no watching, and would appreciate them moving on."

"Nervy, by god."

"True enough. But they up and followed her to her room wanting to go in to check if her husband was in. She turns after opening the door and says for them to leave, that he wasn't in. With a few sarcastic grumbles about seeing to him later, they go down the stairs and out the door. The next day George and a friend pulls up with a wagon, with him underneath some cover just in case, and load up Phoebe and the child for the return to Farmington, then Lincoln."

"Well, it's encouraging to see one of the Coes have some sense, surprising as it is."

"That's what I thought. But rumor has it Al Coe and family is about to follow George."

"Mercy!" astounded Woods.

"And I hear a third Coe, Frank, is thinking the same."

"Lordy! Must be a plague of sensibility striking down the Coe clan!"

"Well, I think it's probably because the New Mexico governor, that Ben Hur fella, done put out rewards on members of both gangs, and also sent up a militia company to look into the possibilities of rounding them up."

"Ben Hur? Oh, you mean Governor Wallace who is writing something called *Ben-Hur*?"

"Aw, hell, you know who I mean."

"Yeah, that's right, I did hear about the militia thing and how it's getting some of the boys nervous up here. If it's true, I hope they run off both gangs. Be an improvement for certain."

"God damn," guffawed Valliant. "Listen to us. If we don't sound like a pair of upright citizens in a Sunday pulpit!"

Woods echoed his laughter with, "Don't let Ike know or we'll be sharing the same tree limb!"

Into the door a moment later galumphed Milt Buchanan and Gus Heffron. Buchanan of course had to let his presence be known with, "Hey! Whar in hell is everybody? How come you got no business in this tomb, Valliant? You ain't shut down, ain't you?"

"No, big mouth, not hardly," replied Valliant. "Just too early in the day to be putting up with riff-raff crawling out of their holes."

"Well, me and Gus have a hellova thirst that's gotta be tended to, if you don't mind breaking away from your puny socializing," retorted Buchanan, as his eyes narrowed on Woods.

Valliant strode over to the bar with the pair of empty bowls and set them on the bar. "What you gents have a thirst for?"

"A couple double shots of whiskey with beer chasers," hailed Buchanan.

Woods grimly chomped the last of his sandwich while he slipped the hammer-thong off his Colt. "I'll have another glass of your wonderful beer, Valliant," he called from across the room as the new customers continued to stand with their backs to him.

Woods hadn't seen Buchanan since their brief confrontation at the Joel Estes' wedding party, and he was certain the obese one hadn't forgotten the odoriferous episode. It also brought back Buchanan's obnoxious mouth; his taunting personal asides, his verbal comments obliquely of Emily Stockton, his public boasting of his readiness to drill George from hidden ambush at the Estes' residence, the vile rumors he spread which helped end Woods' friendship with Joel. It All instantly dumped on his mind the moment he saw Buchanan walk through the door. It locked Woods'temper in a black mode and pierced him with an unsettling rage. He wondered whether Buchanan intentionally dropped in for a showdown knowing he was there. He desperately hoped so with all his quaking heart and turbulent mind; quaking heart because it suddenly brought his old feelings of Emily to surface, and turbulent mind for he deeply desired to eliminate this thorn in his side.

Buchanan's companion, Gus Hefferon, was the one-time side-kick and ranch foreman of Davy Crockett back in Cimarron, who was a distant cousin to the noted Crockett casualty of the Alamo. The two had been shot up by the sheriff of Cimarron and a pair of deputies; Crockett killed and Heffron wounded. Heffron was jailed but escaped two weeks later. Making his way to Durango and being somewhat acquainted with Port and Ike, he continued his colorless career as a member of the Stockton-Eskridge coalition. When Heffron and Buchanan became acquainted it was the case of two sides of the same coin laminating; what one lacked in vacuousness the other would fill in.

As Valliant delivered Woods his beer he added softly, "I know what you intend on doing, George. But not in here. Take him in the street if you got to, though it'd be smarter to let the fool go for now. Pick a better moment. Hell, you know he'll give you one down the road."

"Damn, I hate mind readers. But, Okay. Long as he don't draw first."

As George sat alone at his corner table, he suddenly never felt so alone. A melancholy pall sat upon his shoulders of a sudden as if it had no other place to go. Finding a home, it snuggled up and made itself comfortable. The somberness of the mood soon enveloped his entire body and mind. He suddenly found himself welcoming it like it an old coat and cared not how it blocked the sun, unconcerned as how it drug him down to depths he hadn't visited in many a month, depths which he vowed he'd never return to. But now here he was, and he felt glad. What and why?

It was Emily. His ever sweet Emily. He felt fine up til fat boy walked into the room with his big mouth and his rat-faced friend. It was Buchanan who brought memories of her with his most unwanted presence. Milt had spoken demeaningly and ill of her and George of course never forgot.

Nor would he ever. And the memory of her of a sudden made him realize how much he missed her and how much he still loved her. That is why he believed mister gloom came over to the table and sat on George's head. To make him remember. As if he ever really forgot. Now came the sharp pain of remembering. He knew too he had better get up soon and leave before words were exchanged, words of heat and hate and thunder, or there would be an awful lot of hollered threats and gunsmoke and two men left dead on the floor and Bill Valliant would never forgive him for breaking his word about not killing anyone in his saloon. Yes, he said to himself, looking at the backs of the two joking and chortling fools filling their guts with liquid courage. Depending how much the two already had swilled before coming here, it wouldn't take long. George could already smell the stink of their bogus bravery all the way across the room. As Valliant was pouring them a third pair of double shots he peered between the two bravos and caught George's eye, who shook his head to him in a barely perceived no: don't do it.

George emptied the last of his beer glass, set his hat on his head and stood. He nodded to Valliant with a light smile and walked casually to the front door only a few yards away, keeping his eye on the backs of the standing drinkers. Of the two only Buchanan had his hammer thong loose, obvious of his intent. But then George had also left his still unlooped, just in case. They were only a couple feet away, if that.

"See ya, Bill," farewelled George.

"Take care, ol' buddy."

It was then Buchanan made his move. He stepped back a pace from the bar and twisted toward George, right hand slipping over his holster toward his gun butt. His companion Gus was unaware of his movement, being preoccupied sipping at his shot glass. George swiftly drew and stepped up to whack Bob across the top of his head with the barrel of his Colt with unrestrained enthusiasm. As the fat man dropped to the floor unconscious, inebriated Gus looked down in surprise and joshed, "Damn Milt. Yore drunker than I thought!"

George then reached down and took a fistful of Buchanan's back collar and dragged him toward the front door, commenting to Valliant, "I'll just take the trash out and stack it by the hitchrail, Bill. If that's o.k.?"

"Much appreciated, George," replied the proprietor. "Much appreciated."

After hauling and leaving Buchanan's inert body at the rack, George mounted up and trotted around the corner in a southerly direction down Main Street toward Durango. In six or eight blocks as he was crossing the Animas River bridge he heard a pair of gunshots in the near distance, then a scattering of individuals running about excitedly. Just ahead as he was approaching First and H downtown he saw La Plata Sheriff Barney Watson and deputy Jim Sullivan, their guns drawn and still smoking. They were looking down upon a man twisting and gnashing in excruciating pain on the plank sidewalk. As he pulled up he recognized it was Ike Stockton. Bud Galbreath was manacled and sitting in the bed of a wagon, dispassionately observing Ike's crippled plight.

"Watson, Sullivan," addressed Woods. "You boys okay? You need assistance?"

"We're as smooth as silk, George," retorted Watson. "But seems we could use a litle help, if you wouldn't mind?"

"You got it. Be glad to."

What had culminated so quickly and tragically that noonday began hardly an hour earlier. The incompetent and corrupt sheriff, Luke Hunter, had resigned his office which was taken over by Barney Watson. He in turn appointed Jim Sullivan as his deputy. Although both possessed checkered backgrounds and were echoes of the bandits they pursued, they were looked upon as champions of the law for desiring to rid Ike Stockton's reign in the area. Both too held special contempt for Ike's Judas-capture of Wilkinson for the reward money. Looking ahead, Watson quickly obtained a warrant for Stockton for the murder of rancher Aaron Baker the previous March, and a warrant for Galbreath for rape and murder, and the killing of a deputy in his successful escape from Bosque County, Texas years before.

So the law was waiting when the two wanted men were spotted pulling into Durango and parking their wagon on the corner of First and H. Ike debarked to enter a nearby building while Bud waited in the wagon, having a smoke.

"Howdy, Bud," greeted the sheriff quietly as he shoved a gun in his side. Sullivan slipped next to him to relieve him of his revolver. They snapped the cuffs on him and left him with deputy Jack Wilson to go after Ike, weapons drawn. Ike within moments reappeared in the doorway, spotted the badge-wearers, and jumped back, going for his gun. But Stockton was too foolish and too late, and the sheriff and his deputy fired in unison. Ike was hit in the upper right leg and it shattered, felling him. It is possible both men aimed low for a light wound, looking to take him alive to stand trial for Barker's murder, then hoping he would to be given a legal hanging. If so, perhaps both their bullets struck the same place just below the hip. It was unknown then that he had been given a fatal wound, for the bullet, or bullets, completely fragmentized his upper femur.

As Woods was reining up, Stockton lay flaying and howling in agony.

"Help us load Ike in the wagon, George!"called the sheriff.

Woods dismounted and he and the three lawmen tossed Ike in the bed.

"Bud,"ordered the sheriff. "You and Jack hold him down. Sit on him if you have to, he's outta control with that busted-up leg!"

Stockton, shouting and thrashing from his devastating wound, was fed liberal amounts of liquor to help numb the pain. They then took off south on Main in a wild rush, followed by Woods.

The sheriff surmised the safe thing to do would be to get Ike out of town before the mob, which they knew was forming already, gathered in greater force with their joyous hearts set upon a lynching. The best place would be the San Juan Smelter building which was just being constructed. It was across the Animas River from Durango and a perfect fort. Galloping to beat hell, they made it across the bridge with little time to spare, for the news spread like a conflagration out of control with runners and horsemen alike drawn like flies to offal. Several of the earlier mob members, reliable shooters known to the lawmen, were physically pulled in as additional deputies and used as protectors against the lynchers. Word too was sent out for doctors, and soon there were seven medical men with their little black bags stuffed with knives, saws, tongs, hammers and medical paraphernalia anxious to do their duty under Doctor Henry Ashland Clay.

While the collection of sawbones anesthetized, inspected, conferred and diagnosed their patient, a great part of the region's citizenry seemed to have gathered before the Smelter office shouting, screaming and cursing at the now fairly drugged Stockton. They waved six guns, shotguns, rifles, clubs, rakes and fists, voicing the chant over and over, "Go to hell with Bert Wilkinson!" After about an hour the throng of cheerleading sportsmen trickled down to a herd, then a flock, then finally to a bored handful who grumblingly shuffled back across the Animas River bridge to the nearest saloon to sate a needed thirst as medication for their hoarse throats after all the cheering they had given vent to. By two in the afternoon the vigilante threat dissipated and three lawmen settled in as watchmen with the few extra guardsmen who remained. They had now but to wait for fate to take its course, assisted by the handful of medical experts who were at the crucial moment of their unquestionable and irrefutable decision: the leg must be removed at its shattering point. And it was. Sedated as Ike was, and unconscious as he undoubtedly was also, his body yet rebelled in its reaction to the unbearable pain of cutting and chopping dismemberment to howl and scream in protest, twisting and flopping against the forced strength of several of the surgeons who lay across his body to pin him down. As the hours crept by Ike's violent reaction descended to a series of moans, groans and sighs as his blood loss began to weaken him, and the sedation kindly took firmer hold.

Across the room aloofly observing the medicos stood Ike's wife, the lovely and diminutive 23-year-old Amanda Ellen Robinson Stockton. Next to her on either side clutching her in confusion, fear and fright were her two offspring, Delilah, six, sobbing in terror, and Guy, eighteen months. Amanda stood stoically through the entire bloody ordeal, listening to the whispered conferences, watching the removal of the leg, holding and softly shushing her two trembling children, whose faces were soaked with tears. Several of the deputies would look over now and then in admiration at her inner strength, in awe at the calm demeanor she displayed, standing as a statue of steel with protective arms about her offspring. She had arrived with her children in a small wagon pulled by a horse, driving straight through the mob of ranters looking neither left nor right, not caring who in hell might be run over. She pulled up at the door of the office, jumped out, gathered her kids and strut into the building as if she owned the place. She remained where she stood now, not moving or saying a word. The sheriff and his deputy, both knowing Ike, walked over earlier to deliver their condolences with hats in hand. She nodded wordlessly, and they left her alone. George noticed her outright as she sped through the clustered mass of screeching and cursing fools, practically running them down as they parted like the Red Sea, realizing it was Ike's wife and children.

But hell, before he could make a move to help her she was out of the wagon and into the building, ignoring the hoard of mindless yahoos around her. He too had instant admiration for her courage in plowing through that jungle of brainless mankind. She was tiny, but mighty.

The afternoon frittered away until at five o'clock Woods took his courage in hand and respectfully strode over to address Ellen Stockton who stood rock-like with her arms about her offspring. Removing his hat he inquired, "Please excuse me, Missus Stockton, but if you and the children would like something to eat, I would be more than glad to have dinner brought in."

Ellen looked Woods in the eyes and replied, "Thank you. That's most kind of you. A sandwich would suffice for me, and some water. But I'm certain the children must be starved."

"What would you two like to eat?" inquired Woods, kind and soft as he could, knowing the shock they must be in.

The pair merely clung tighter to their mother for security and safety, her daughter now quieted, having a natural fear of this stranger with a gun on his hip and a rifle in his hand.

"Some soup," whispered Guy shyly. "And cake. Chocolate cake."

"Oh, Guy," smiled his mother. "That surely sounds delicious! I think I'll have some too!"

"What I'll do, maam, is to see a food run is made for all of us. I'll be back shortly."

"Thank you," replied Ellen. "That would be most kind."

Woods, with the sheriff and his deputy, made up a food list for all concerned since no one had a bite to eat before noon. Sheriff Watson gave the order to a pair of deputies with instructions, "And you tell him the bill will be taken care of by the law soon as this is over. Include two-dozen bottles of beer, too."

By the time the men returned Woods had found a small table and three chairs for Ellen and her children. Soon he brought in sandwiches, heated stew, some cake (chocolate), soft drinks and a canteen of water. Dragging another chair over, he joined them in the small repast. It was near seven p.m. when all had eaten, and the atmosphere between the four had mellowed somewhat.

Ike was quite silent now, having not made a sound in several hours. Woods paid the doctors a brief visit for news, but they could say nothing definite, except that he had slipped into a coma from shock and loss of blood. Optimistic, they felt maybe with some rest he may pull through.

Returning to the seated trio, Woods passed on the positive comment of the doctor, that he may pull through now with some rest.

Ellen retorted to the words with a cold stare. "Well, I come here not to see him live. I am awaiting his hoped-for demise."

Woods himself had no love for Ike whatsoever, but thought as a wife she would be a shade more remorseful. She continued in a cold recitation of facts and comment, neither in condemnation nor judgement.

"He was a vile creature who had no right putting me through years of lies and deceit. His endless plans for a cattle ranch was all talk, mere pies in the sky, and I believed him since I was a sixteen-year-old bumpkin blinded by the romance of his descriptions. After a few years I saw he was nothing but a rustler, killer and thief, with a mouth filled with fraud, trickery and deception. He and Porter were the two sides of the same coin, although Ike was the more clever manipulator. No, I want to leave here a widow, if I have to run over and pull all them bandages off him by myself. He has spread enough misery around for a dozen lifetimes, and it is time for him to go."

Woods remained mute, struck speechless by such unemotional honesty he had never been witness to before.

"You are the George Woods who was sweet on Emily Stockton, are you not?"

"Uh, yes maam."

"I must say you had treated her most decently, Mister Woods, and she much appreciated your kindnesses in her bereaved state. I did too. Not many men treat women as thoughtful and respectful. I can surely testify to that."

"Uh, um, you're too kind, maam. I'm just glad Emily found some happiness with Joel. She more than deserved it. He's a good man."

"Yes, he is. And yes, she did. And hopefully before the night is up a touch of happiness will also be mine."

The talk of Emily brought back familiar thumps in his heart, and that warm feeling of soft love at a distance which never died. He hoped all was going well with her. He had never heard much of Ellen except through Emily's comments now and then, and knew she and Ike were not the happiest couple in town.

The hours crawled by slowly now, and by nine o'clock all the physicians left but one. There was little to do now but to keep watch as to his progress. Woods left the Stockton trio for a walk in the night air. The weary children were curled up in blankets on the floor while their mother sat and awaited the outcome of her chances for happiness. She strolled over once near ten to inquire of the doctor how the patient was fairing.

"His pulse is very slow and weak, Missus Stockton. But he's still bravely holding on. We can but wait and hope."

"Yes," came her grim comment. "I am certainly waiting and hoping."

"Well, madam," he sympathized. "I will hope with you also. And pray the good Lord sees fit to return Mister Stockton to your side in his most merciful manner."

She nodded her head and looked down upon the blanket-wrapped body and pale face of her unconscious spouse, heavy beads of perspiration across his forehead. He looked thinner, nearly gaunt from his long torment. More yellow than white, and with a tinge of green. Maybe some wishes do come true, she thought, as she turned and walked back to the table and patiently sat.

Woods, breathing in the night air felt refreshed, the confined room reeking of medicinal smells and the subtle odor of rotting flesh.

"Anything new out here, Jim?" he asked of Sullivan, standing with a Winchester in hand.

"Naw. The brave lynch mob is in town drinking and bragging and braying over Ike's lost leg. I was hoping someone would squeeze off a shot. I wanted so bad to drill that loudmouthed leader Pat Stanley I almost cried when nobody had the balls to trigger off a round. Had him in my sights near an hour."

"Yeah. You can see a couple saloons all lit up from here. Best night they've had since the Wilkinson hanging."

"All the docs that left don't give Ike much of a chance. Guess we busted him up a good one. They don't think he'll survive the night."

"Think you're right. His wife's taking it stoutly."

"I'll say. I honestly don't think Ike deserved that pretty little filly. Good looking kids, too."

"Certainly are."

Equally moved, a reporter described Ellen as "a refined and gentle woman."

Woods walked toward the riverbank in the high waning moonlight, standing at the edge and listening to the softly gurgling water as it slid south into New Mexico only a hop away. He wanted to be alone for a time to clear his head, take his mind away from Ellen who was filling it more than he could believe, being drawn to her. What the devil was he thinking of, anyway? A beauty she was, and keen-minded as well. Bitter, but no fool. Somewhere Emily and Ellen shifted places. Ellen was the needful one now, and his yearning for Emily overlapped to reach out gradually to Ellen since he began talking to her. God, she was a sweet looking woman.

Returning to the office he looked at his watch: midnight. Going over to the doctor he asked softly, "Any change for the better, doc?"

"Afraid not, George. Pulse getting very faint. Don't say anything to his missus, but I doubt he'll make it til sunup."

Woods walked across the room to Ellen's side, her face startlingly lovely in its angelic paleness, although drawn from the hours of waiting. He felt a strong desire to tenderly take her in his arms to console her, ease her acetic acrimoniousness. Taking the chair next to her he asked, "Why don't you curl up with a blanket for a nap next to your young 'uns? I'll notify you of any change in Ike."

"No, George. I couldn't sleep if I tried. I notice you speaking to the doctor. What did he have to say?"

If it were anyone else he would have soft-pedaled the doctor's words. But he knew she'd know and probably curse him for it. "His pulse is quite weak. The doc doubts he'll see daylight."

"Thank you. I appreciate your honesty and the good news."

Why did he also feel glad? It was the old aching need, the old food, the blood in his heart needing fresh drink. Emily. He missed her so, didn't realize how much until fat boy entered Valliant's yesterday afternoon. And so enchanting was the call for new love: Ellen. Overtired, he was soon half-slumping in his chair forcing himself to remain alert and awake between his musings over Emily and Ellen. His thoughts were fractured fragments of confused fantasies, fleeting pieces of dusty wishes. Nodding between waking and sleeping, her voice summoned him from afar.

". . . now, George."

"What?" he asked, wiping the web of drowsiness from his eyes. "I'm sorry, Ellen. I must have fallen asleep."

"I said, he's dead. It's over now, George. All but the burying."

He raised his head to see the doctor walking away toward the blanket-wrapped corpse. He had brought word to Ellen of Ike's passing. George looked at his watch: 2:43 a.m.

"I'm sorry," he mumbled, feeling hypocritical.

"I must go now," she smiled all afresh. "It has been a wonderful pleasure talking to you, George. You must come visit sometime. Anytime after the burial. Please." Then she and the children were gone.

Isaac Thomas Stockton.
(29 Feb 1852-27 Sep 1881.)

Courtesy Frederick Nolan

Smoke stack remains of San Juan & New York Mining and Smeltering Company,
now also obliterated. Site of Ike Stockton's demise. Animas River in foreground.

Photo, J. S. Peters.

Ike Stockton grave marker
Should read, Sep 27.

Photo, J. S. Peters.

George W. Kephart, merchant. Mayor of Durango late 1890s.
Wounded by Port Stockton, 1881. Photo, Jim Davenport.

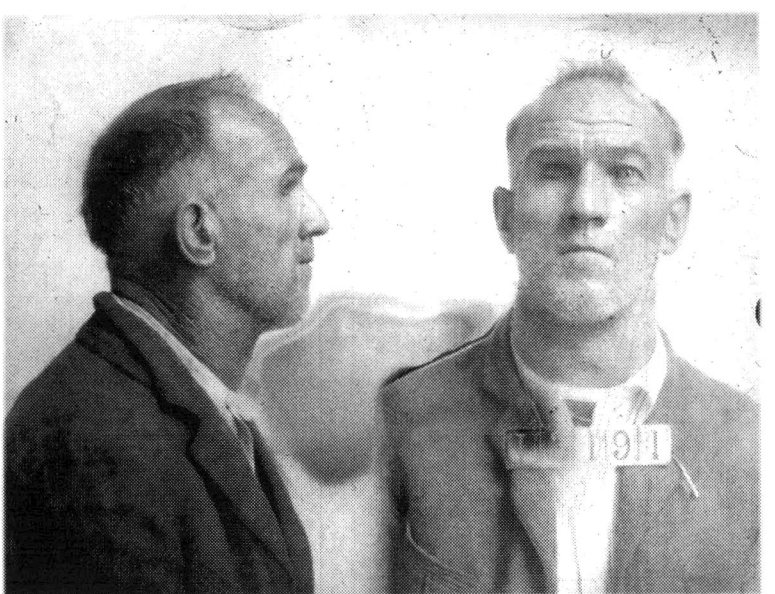

Mug shots of Cleveland Estes, #13191.   Colorado State Archives, Denver Col.

Salt Lake City, Utah, November 22nd, 1920

Application of CLEVE ESTES

To the Honorable Board of Pardons of the State of Utah:

I hereby apply to your Honorable Body for a Re-hearing and respectfully represent as follows:

First—That I am serving a term of imprisonment in Utah State Prison under conviction and a sentence on a charge of Second Degree Murder

Second—I was convicted and sentenced on the 22 day of April A. D. 1917, at Montecello County of San Jaun and State of Utah, in Seventh District Court, in and for the County and State aforesaid, Honorable Judge Christensen presiding

Third—I was sentenced to Fifteen (15) years

and thereafter was imprisoned in the Utah State Prison

Fourth—Honorable Knox Patterson prosecuted the case.

Fifth—My true name in full is Cleve Estes

I was convicted under the name of Cleve Estes

Sixth—The names of persons charged to have been connected with the same offense are as follows: None

Seventh—I have never been convicted of any offense except None

Respectfully submitted,

Cleve Estes

Cleve Este's request for re-hearing. Courtesy, Monte Pruett.

Salt Lake City, Utah, _July 7_ 1916

Application of _A. H. Wilmot_

To the Honorable Board of Pardons of the State of Utah:

I hereby apply to your Honorable Body for a _Pardon_ and respectfully represent as follows:

First—That I am serving a term of imprisonment in _the Harris Co jail_ under conviction and sentence on a charge of _Petty Larceny_

Second—I was convicted and sentenced on the _15_ day of _May_ A. D. _1916_, at _330_ County of _Harris_ and State of Utah, in _Justice_ Court, in and for the County and State aforesaid, Honorable _Judge Harias_ presiding.

Third—I was sentenced to _One hundred days or_ _$100 dolar fine have Payed $1800 cash_ and thereafter was imprisoned in the _10 days in Jail_

Fourth—Honorable _Harris_ prosecuted the case.

Fifth—My true name in full is _Acy H Wilmot_ I was convicted under the name of _Acy H Wilmot_

Sixth—The names of persons charged to have been connected with the same offense are as follows: _George Clark_

Seventh—I have never been convicted of any offense except _none what ever_

Joseph C Hadler, 360 W 7th South St
Edward Johnson; Salt Lake City

Respectfully submitted,

A H Wilmot

Acy Wilmot's application for a pardon.   Courtesy, Monte Puett.

No 4720
Warranty Deed
Isaac Pye
To
Geo. H. Wood.
Filed for Record
at 1st O'clock P.M.
January 13, 1882.
Robt J Carson
Recorder
By A. S. Bradley Dpy.

This Indenture, Made this 15th day of January in the Year of our Lord One Thousand Eight hundred and eight hundred and eighty two, between Isaac Pye of the County of La Plata and State of Colorado, of the first part, and George H Wood of the same County and State of the second part. Witnesseth: That the said party of the first part for and in consideration of the sum of One Thousand Dollars to him duly paid, has sold and by these presents does Grant, Bargain, Sell and convey to the said party of the second part, his heirs and assigns, all the tract or parcel of land, situated in La Plata County, and State of Colorado, and described as follows, viz:

The East One half (½) of the North East One fourth (¼) Section fifteen (15) and North West One fourth ¼ of North West One fourth (¼) of Section No fourteen (14) in Township Thirty five (35) North of Range No Nine (9) West N.M.M containing One hundred and Twenty acres.

To Have and To Hold the same, with all the appurtenances, and all the estate, right, title and interest of the said party of the first part therein; And the said Isaac Pye do hereby covenant and agree, that at the delivery hereof he the said Isaac Pye is the lawful owner of the premises above granted and seized of a good and indefeasible estate of Inheritance, In fee simple, free and clear of all incumbrances whatsoever, and that he will Warrant and Defend the same and every part thereof, in the quiet and peaceable possession of said party of the second part, his heirs and assigns forever.

In Witness Whereof, The said party of the first part has hereunto set his hand and seal the day and year above written.
Isaac Pye
By his Attorney in fact [Seal]
Jas. O Harris [Seal]

George Wood's land purchase, 13 Jan. 1882.
Courtesy Julie Pickett

George Wood's Baptismal Certificate. Notation: "Executed in Durango for murder, June 23, 1882. Was converted and baptized a few minutes before his execution. MCB." Courtesy Julie Pickett.

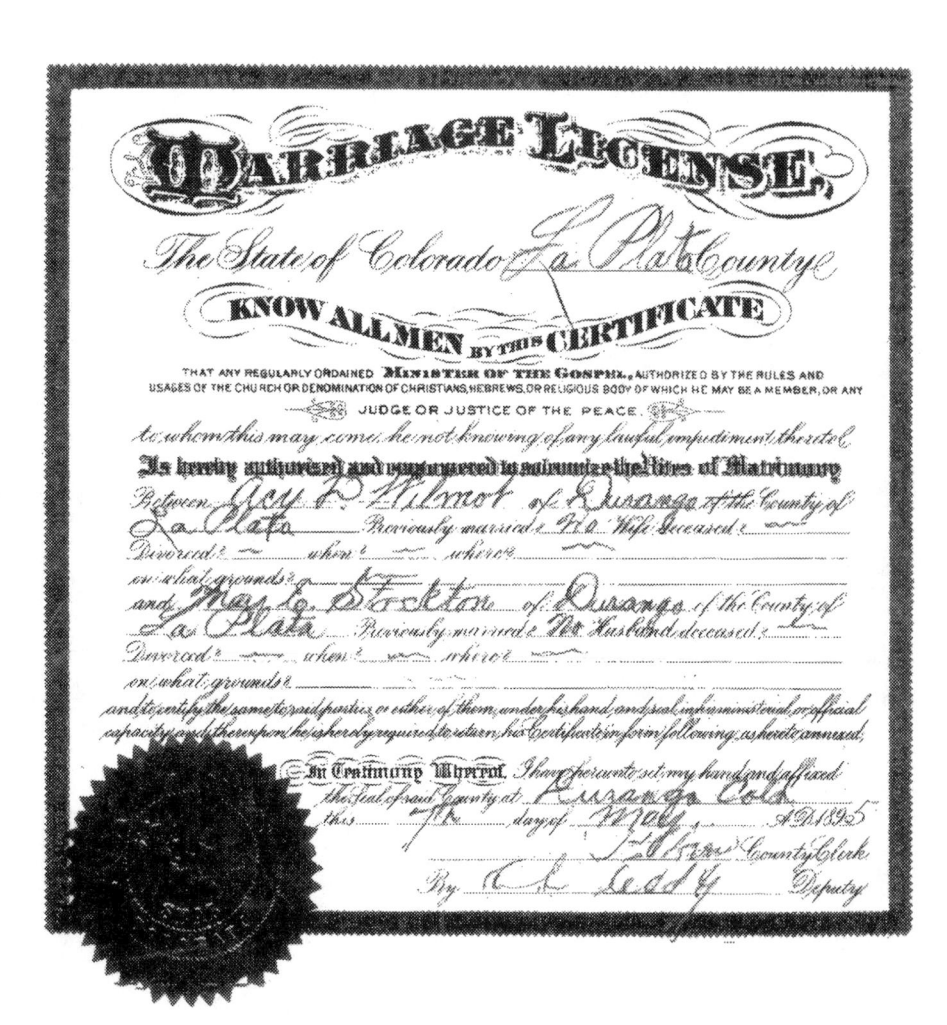

Acy D. Wilmot and May E. Stockton marriage certificate.
Courtesy Julie Pickett.

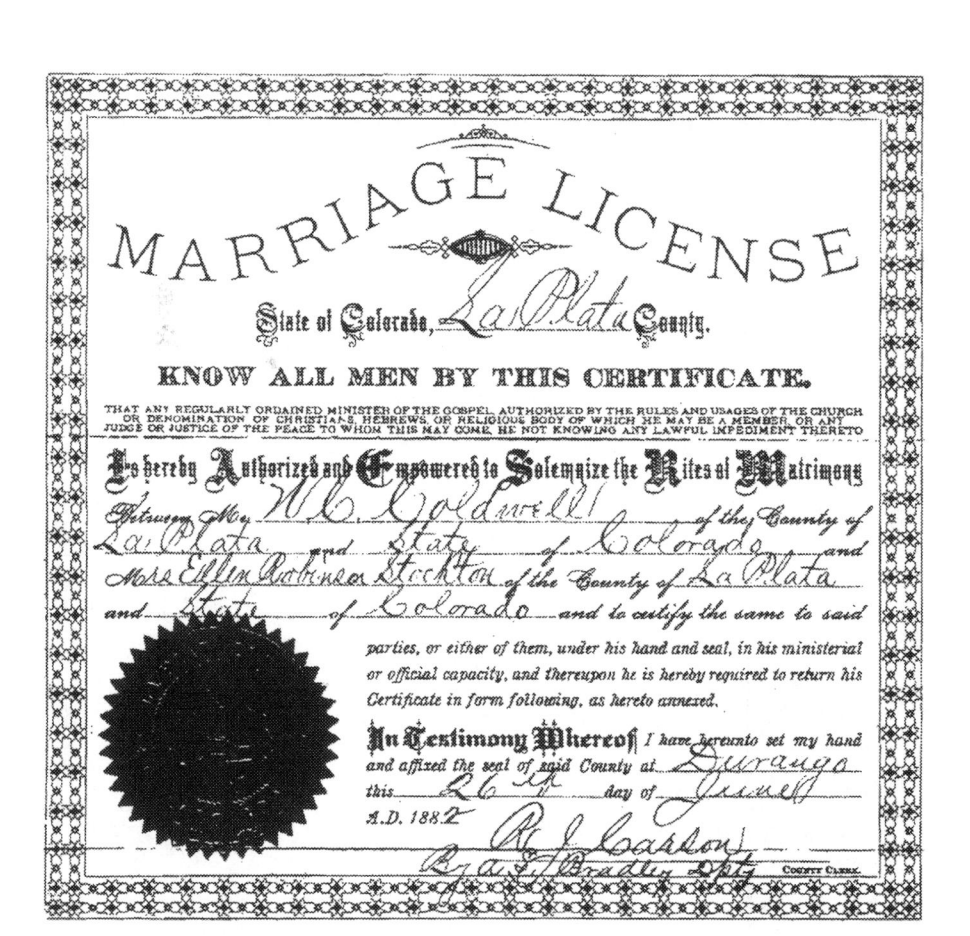

N. C. Coldwell and Ellen Robinson marriage certificate. Courtesy Julie Pickett

A. R. Johnson and Sarah Ellen Stockton marriage certificate. Courtesy Julie Pickett.

Sarah Ellen Stockton, Durango, circa 1891.

Courtesy Pam Birmingham.

Richard Francis Sheeran and Sarah Ellen Stockton, Denver, circa, 1895.   Courtesy Pam Birmingham.

Quartet celebrating St. Paddy's Day in Durango, circa 1900.
Richard Francis Sheeran standing right.

Courtesy Pam Birmingham.

Sarah Ellen Sheeran seated with granddaughter;
daughter standing.   Courtesy Pam Birmingham.

Sarah Ellen Stockton Johnson, Brea, California, 1930. Courtesy Pam Birmingham.

"Son and daughter of Isaac Thomas Stockton." Courtesy Gail Kaufmann.

Guy Stockton (Jan 1880-15 Mar 1932). Delilah Stockton (28 Dec 1874-31 Jan 1963).

TWENTY

The killing of Ike Stockton appeared to have helped the beginning of clearing out the strutting gunsels from the Durango area, and was looked upon as a blessing by many of the locals. Lawmen Watson and Sullivan, whatever their faults or virtues, let it be known they would brook no nonsense from any tin horn trouble maker within shooting distance, and the flocks of turkeys took wing not caring to put the two to the test.

Charlie Allison took a handful of followers south into New Mexico, hurrahing, shooting and robbing several tiny Colorado villages on their way out. Deputy Sheriff Frank Hyatt of Conejos, Colorado immediately took a train south after them to Santa Fe. In Alburquerque, Hyatt, with a small posse, nabbed Allison, Lew Perkins and Henry Watts without a shot.

The Eskridge brothers, choosing survival, took to the road; one to San Diego, it was said.

The three Coes and their families returned to southern New Mexico where they took up honest farming and ranching, and proudly displayed themselves as pioneers.

The gunman-rancher Simmons, acknowledged leader of the Farmington faction of rustlers, was shot to death near Flora Vista, New Mexico.

Big Dan Howland was said to have died attached to a rope later in Tombstone, Arizona for killing a man in Bisbee.

Even the dangerous Tom Nance saw the weather change and pulled out (after he slashed William "Big Bill" Thompson across the gut in a poker game). Years later, on a Sunday night of mid-September 1892, he met his end in a bar fracas in Holbrook, Arizona where he was brutally kicked to death by herder J. B. Mitchell.

Some of the locals who were not head-liners but mere horse-handlers or occasional cow-catchers stayed put, but kept a low profile and found honest jobs, never to mention or boast of their grey past evermore, except possibly to each other over a beer when meeting now and then over the years to quietly boast or swap stories of, "the good ol' days."

George, in irony, was staying of late at a small farm out of town on the Animas River with John Cowen, Emily's 43-year-old brother. A widower, he had a son William, 16, and a daughter Lizzie, 14. John and he met one afternoon in town not a week before Ike's shooting. Both had earlier been part-time cattle collectors for the Stocktons, but had quit. Chatting awhile, John asked if George were free to do some carpentry work at his place for room and board and a few bucks.

"Yessiree, John. Just happened to finish up a job yesterday, and be glad to."

A further irony was that the Ike Stocktons lived only two houses away. George had never met Ellen as yet, and had never been to Ike's home, although knowing the Cowens and Stocktons were neighbors. George threw himself into building several sheds and a chicken coop for Cowen, who was expanding to hogs, chickens and eggs. George's trip to Durango the day Ike got shot up was a day off he happened to take.

Twenty-nine-year-old Isaac Thomas Stockton was interred in the hilly Animas City Cemetery just outside of town on 28 September at 2 p.m. Parson C.M. Hoge gave a small and touching eulogy before the small gathering who attended, including Ellen and her children, and Emily and Joel Estes.

TWENTY ONE

Four days following Ike's burial, on the sunny afternoon of 2 October, George Woods, after a bath and change into clean underwear, clean white shirt, shined boots, only suit and brushed beaver hat, rode in a circuitous route from the Cowen's to Ellen's house. Tying his horse beneath one of many shade trees, he removed his hat and nervously knocked. When Ellen opened the door with a radiant smile and a, "Oh, George! I am so happy to see you," he was completely spellbound as he was exposed to pure, ravishing beauty. Having brushed her jet-black hair to her shoulders, Ellen was wearing a low-cut, rose-flowered, short-sleeved dress hemmed just below her knees, and stood barefoot. He swam in the pools of her shimmering dark eyes glowing just for him.

"Please, George," she welcomed. "Please do come in. I've been looking forward so to your visit!"

Walking on a cloud, he moved through the door into a tastefully decorated home. The crazy thought hit him that this could not possibly be the home of a gunman's wife. Widow, he corrected. He stood in the center of the front room looking about in a daze. Turning to her and at a loss for words, he blurted that the place had a nice homey atmosphere.

"I'm so glad you like it. I'm always doing home decoration of some kind. Changing furniture around and things like that. Let me take your coat and hat so you can relax, George. The children are spending the week at Emily and Joel's, so we have the place to ourselves. Please sit. I'll get us some lemonade."

George surrendered his jacket and hat then sat on the divan, listening to Ellen moving about in the kitchen. The place to themselves.

Is that what she said? Lord, she was so different from the embittered wife of before. Widowhood became her, as if she was freed of unnatural anger.

She reentered the room with a pitcher of lemonade and two tall glasses on a tray which she placed on the coffee table before George.

"I do hope you have come with a great thirst!" she chirped.

"Yes, maam, I have. And I thank you."

She leaned forward to enthusiastically and artfully pour juice into their glasses, and as he looked over he saw how low-cut the bodice of her lovely dress was. His unrestricted vision was of a pair of perfectly firm and freely-suspended pink-tipped breasts. George's eyes were as saucers while his mind and body was gripped by an almost unbearable burst of heat. Ellen smiled upon her gawking guest and commented sweetly, "There is more juice in the kitchen whenever you are ready, George. And if you would like, some cake and freshly made bread. I can also make us something to eat. Please don't be shy now."

"Oh, no, maam, I mean yes, but I'm not exactly hungry at the moment. Just thirsty, thank you!"

He quickly drained his glass in several long swallows, then refilled it in a rush, then drank the second half-way.

"My, you *are* thirsty, George!" she laughed lightly, as she plopped next to him, dress high above her knees.

"Yes, yes I was, but I feel better now, ma'am, really!"

"Oh, George, do forget the formalities, please? You know my name is Ellen, so please call me so."

"Oh, yes, ma'am. I mean, Ellen. That I will."

George was too flustered and agog to make any sense for the good part of fifteen minutes, wiping his brow with his handkerchief over and over, and commenting endlessly on how flavorful her lemonade tasted.

As she rose from the divan Ellen said, "That window across the room is awful bright on our eyes, George, don't you think?"

She walked over and pulled the white-laced curtains together to soften the glaring light of the late setting sun. As she stretched up to do so, Woods was re-stunned by another delectable sight. Ellen's dress was of a thin gauzy material which exposed his eyes to her fleshy silhouette, pleasantly proving to his suspicion she wore nothing underneath.

"Now," she asked as she turned toward him. "Is that less blinding, George? It appeared so disturbing to me."

Her frontal outline was even more breathtaking, and her pert breasts and thick pubes seemed to thrust themselves in a tantalizing invitation.

"Yes," he agreed hypnotically. "The glare is certainly gone."

Sliding next to him she cooed, "I do hope you don't think ill of me over the awful things I said of Ike. But life with him was the worse time I have ever experienced."

"Oh, no, Ellen. Everyone knows how harsh he could sometimes be."

"And you are so different, George," she purred. "Really."

Her words were spellbinding, her presence bewitching, and he found himself at sea again.

Over the following weeks as he tried often to recall everything that happened that afternoon and evening, it all seemed a dream, an invention of his imagination. It was as if he were in a slow moving mirage of the senses, hazily entangled in a cluster of arms, legs, lips, mouths and tongues, and he found himself longing more for the dream than the reality.

TWENTY TWO

George Woods never left Ellen Stockton's home until the following afternoon. She was in his arms the moment he finished his second glass of juice, and they melted into each other as natural as butter and toast. An hour after sundown they shifted from the divan to the bedroom, and beneath a flickering candlelight continued lustfully assailing each other. They both were sensually famished, so brought to the sheets pent-up passion primed for thorough release.

Woods again was in love, for Ellen had set him free from his feelings for Emily. He was now in emotional free-flight, liberated from an unrequited passion, finally in the arms of the one whom he truly believed he had been searching for.

Ellen, more cooly pragmatic in her reasoning, had been maritally and emotionally unhappy. She had wished for years to be released from the burdensome yoke of what became a loveless union. Ike's passing gave her the freedom she sought, and Woods, who unwittingly put himself in harm's way, became the opportune lab rat for her calculating persona to test this new sense of unrestraint. Too, there was a taint of jealousy in her over Emily's seemingly contented love-life throughout the years. First Port, whom Emily adored as he did her; then being concernedly tended to by a love-sick George following her being wounded; and finally her happy marriage to Joel Estes. Her envy centered around at how easy and simple Emily's love-life appeared. She wondered too whether she and George had ever been lovers, getting green-eyed over that also, although Emily constantly denied it. But after Woods too vowed it was all a platonic relationship, she accepted it as true. Yet she symbolically notched her bedpost anyway with him as her first trophy, feeling triumphant over Emily, as if it were a contest of competitive copulation.

For several months they continued their affair, but she made George promise to keep it to himself. Whatever her reason, he acquiesced happily; but then he would have agreed to anything, as long as they were together. With her children home again, and with unscheduled visitors coming and going, they rendezvoused three times a week some miles away in the hilly geography of obscure timbers. It was a perfect setting for Woods' besotted mental state; the fluttering and twittering birds, occasional deer or two, soft rays of the sun filtering through the trees. Their private Eden, he mused. Adam and Eve never had it better, even with winter coming on.

There were still times when he could spend a night with her, but that was only if she were alone. A mile away on a low bluff Woods would ride every day, and with his binoculars scope out her bedroom window. If a vase of flowers showed itself there in all its glory, he would ride in after dark, park his steed in the barn, spend the night, and leave before dawn. At long last, love seemed to favor George Woods.

But alas, as some claim, true love never runs smooth. Or as an earlier observer of the human romantic condition concluded, true love is a ghost. And, whichever article came first, the heart, mind or soul, Ellen gradually unraveled herself from all three. Her lab experiment was over. More to the point, she had made the acquaintance of a new man in town, the somewhat striking criminal attorney from Arkansas, Nathaniel Colbert Coldwell. Also most delightfully, the 27-year-old lawyer was an allegeable bachelor. From the first moment they met he was smitten by this naive, incapable, kittenish lovely, and automatically reached out to be her rescuer and protector. He pursued her vigorously as she calculatingly assisted him by reeling in her catch.

Consequently, Woods once again was assigned to canoe the River Styx without a paddle in black angst as Ellen explained one snow-chilled evening in late January, barely a month into the New Year of 1882, that she was betrothed to lawyer Nathaniel Coldwell.

"I heartily want to thank you for the wonderful times we had, George. You are the most wonderful man I have ever known. Know too that you have completely revived my life from the bitter brew I had once drank, and no longer do so, and look with warmer eyes upon the world. Mister Coldwell has offered me a good and comfortable life with him, George, a life that is also a wonderful chance for my children. Please understand. And I know I can trust you as a gentleman of honor to keep secret our clandestine activity these past months."

Riding off into the gelid night, her words fell upon his head like the salutation of an executioner. *And there goes the 120 acres he bought for a thousand dollars just weeks ago,* he thought grimly. *A wedding surprise shot to hell.*

TWENTY THREE

Much water had passed under the bridge since Woods' brief affair with Ellen, and from his point of view, most of it murky. Although still working with the Cowans as a live-in handyman, he was looking about for a change of residence, if not a geographical relocation. For things had gotten quite muddy. It was now the lovely month of April, and a sunny mid-morning found Woods riding north through downtown Durango toward Animas City and Valliant's Saloon.

After Ellen had given him the gate, he moped about until finding himself drawn toward John Cowan's daughter, Lizzie, with his blessing. Now blossoming into an attractive fifteen-year-old, the two were in each other's company often enough for Woods to be looked upon as an extended family member. The relationship, unheated, and mostly in the hand-holding category, was enough to give George's heart a rest, for which it was not only ready but thankful.

Suddenly, slowly at first, then spreading like wildfire, gossip and rumor blanketed the countryside. Woods was at a loss at trying to understand what was taking place. The region had it, even the papers, much to his amazement, that he and Milt Buchanan both pursued Ellen jealously. Shortly after, he ran into Buchanan in Durango one afternoon while on a run to pick up some building material and spoke critically of it to him. The result was a furious argument where Woods ended challenging him to a fist-fight then and there. Buchanan, egged on by booze and anger at embarrassed memories of their past confrontations, drew his Bowie knife and retorted, "No fists, George. No guns, either. Let's see what you're made of. Need a knife?"

Woods merely put his hands on his hips and snarled disgustingly, "Why you fat-assed third-rate butcher. Go peel a pig. You aren't man enough to know what a fist fight is."

He then turned and walked away, disappointing the gathered crowd which looked forward to the contest.

Soon word floated about that Joel Estes claimed Woods had mistreated Emily. Woods replied to the claim that it was Emily who had treated him unfairly. Over what, no one specified. Trash-talk and accusations cut back and forth until it was difficult to know who actually said what. Then Lizzie for some reason pulled away from George, not wanting even social contact with him.

"Damn, John," he complained to Cowan one day. "What is wrong with women? You know me and Lizzie had been nothing but the best of friends, and were well-taken with each other. Now all these tales and stories, that are mostly lies, have of a sudden covered the country like a plague."

"Oh, hell, George. Don't put no stock in all that bullshit. Sounds like frustrated womanhood at work. Who in hell can understand a woman's mind anyways?"

Still puzzled, Woods thought he'd take a ride out to visit Bill Valliant, whom he hadn't seen in a while. Maybe some jawing with him would settle his mind.

As he entered the empty saloon, a surprised Valliant called out, "Christ, George, where in hell you been? Ain't seen you near three months!"

"Perdition," groused Woods.

"What?"

"I said, with your *permission,* I would like to order a glass of beer."

"You got it."

The bar being empty of customers, Woods howled in imitation of Milt Buchanan months ago, "Hey! Whar in hell is everybody? How come you got no business in this tomb, Valliant? You ain't shut down, ain't you?"

Valliant burst out in a roar of laughter at the perfect mimicking of Milt. "Damn, George, it's good to see you ain't lost your sense of humor!"

"So how's about some of that good stew? I'm about starved!"

"O.k. Grab our corner table and I'll be with you in a minute."

In a brief time Valliant joined him with bowls of buffalo stew, tortillas and a pair of beers.

"Business really light?" queried Woods.

"Yeah, it is. With a bunch of the bad ol' boys scurrying out of town and some Animas City businesses moving down the road to Durango, things've slowed a bit. Mostly have afternoon and evening imbibers, so I'm thinking of opening around noon or one. So how's everything going your way? Still at John Cowans?"

"Oh, yeah. But thinking of moving on. Maybe out of town."

"Really? Hell, I've always looked on you as a permanent fixture of this burg. What's wrong?"

"I'm sure you've heard some of the lies that have been flooding the place."

"Sure, heard some. But a lot of us know it's all a bunch of crap."

"And Milt and I almost got into it again."

"After I heard that I knew for certain he's looking for an early grave. And he's spreading the word he's out to kill you."

"I know. So before things get any further out of hand I thought I'd move on out."

"Hate to see you do that, George. To be run off by common gossip and a big mouth. Don't seem right."

"Right? Bill, you can't fight what you can't see. And when people would rather believe the worst they hear of someone than ignore common dirt for what it is, it's a lost cause."

Valliant sat pondering in silence a moment as if measuring the weight of words on his mind.

"George, how long we been friends? Four, five years?"

"At least."

"I got to speak to you of something. Something important. But you got to hear me out and put some thought behind it."

"Well, sure."

"And keep it between us, as personal information."

"My word is good as gold with you, Bill. You know that."

"All right, here it is. A lot of that bull was spread by Ike's widow, Ellen. Most of the town know you and her been carrying on all winter, no matter how quiet you two were about it. You were seen going back and forth to her place often, sly as you tried to be. Anyway, Ellen knew that sooner or later her lawyer-fiancé would hear of it, so wrote a few letters explaining you were only a slight acquaintance continuously after her, using harsh and insulting language because she rebuffed you."

"Good god, Bill! I told her she had nothing to worry about. That she could trust my word."

"She don't run on trust, George. She runs on fear. And the fear of losing her lawyer-love made her paint you black. She even whispered to Fat Boy's ear that you used nasty words at her, and so of course he picked up the gauntlet like a good knight."

"Good Christ, Bill. How in the world did you come by this information?"

"A close woman friend who is a friend of Ellen's. Was, that is. They had a falling out about it."

Woods sat stunned, although he did suspect the possibility of Ellen protecting her future marital interest. But back then he shelved the thought, thinking his anger was getting the best of him.

"Jesus, Bill," he groaned, blushing like a fool. "It all fits. I feel like I've been standing on a trap door with her hand on the lever. I'm just . . . . what? Disappointed? Disgusted? Disenchanted? Damn if I know. I'm numb. Maybe I was just plain stupid in the first place."

TWENTY FOUR

For the rest of April George Woods moved about as if underwater, almost in a dream, wondering at his alternatives. He actually had but two: go or stay. He could leave all this mess behind him, fork his mount for a long ride elsewhere, free from all this nonsense. Or stay. Then what? For more foolishness? If he remained he and Milt would have it out, with Milt leaving the arena feet-first. And that might lead to more trouble, unless it were solidly self-defense. Or too, he could be neatly dry-gulched some dark night, which he would not put past the fat one.

What sank him into a deeper funk was that John Cowan suddenly ended their friendship and evicted him from the house, then sent Lizzie off to a Catholic school in Trinidad. No amount of pleading could change Cowan's mind. It was made up soon as he heard the contents of one of Ellen's latest letters. Crushed, George moved out, taking a room in town. He was now becoming a nervous wreck, desperately grabbing at a thousand mental straws in the hopes of finding a solution to his monstrous dilemma. Sleep evaded him; food was of no importance; the hours became agony.

April came and went. On May Day he completed a few lingering chores, then set his mind on leaving for Trinidad the next day.

Sleeping late the following morning, he rose, shaved, cleaned up, then packed what few belongings he had in a old valise. But then he made up his mind to have a final word or two with Ellen before departing this place forever. Yes. It would settle his head greatly to say a few things to her that needed airing. Or, maybe he could try and reason with her? What was there to lose?

Dismounting before her house he pounded more than knocked at her door, growing more mentally heated then he meant to be along his ride. When she opened the door she was surprised to see him.

"George," she cut in a scolding tone. "What in hell are you doing here?"

That did it. She was no longer the sweetheart he had seen and held so often in his arms, but a harsh, insensitive scold.

"God damn you, you black-hearted bitch! You were the one turned Lizzie against me! And sending those letters to people, including Emily, writing all that lying trash about me to make you look so innocent and saintly because you were scared I'd tell your lawyer-love about our months of screwing! You deceptive bitch!"

"Get your ass to hell out of here George Woods, you crazy bastard! Get out!"

Ellen then reached for a Winchester just inside the door which brought some sense of sanity to Woods' mind, and he lit for his horse. As he raced away clinging to his mount's neck, making him low in the saddle, he heard several shots and in moments the angry hissing of bullets speeding by his ears like bees for honey.

The following day Ellen pressed charges. The complaint read, "George N. Woods on the 2nd of May did willfully disturb the peace and quiet of the family of Mrs. A. E. Stockton by tumultuous and offensive carriage, and by threatening, traducing and quarreling with her, the said Mrs. A. E. Stockton." Losing his temper played right into her hands.

Twenty days later, on 23 April, Woods appeared in court. He was indicted to appear before the Grand Jury at the next term, and bonded out at $250. Fred Steinger posted bond for him and appointed a pair of attorneys for his defense.

Just prior to his hearing, Cap Flagler, a lawyer and ex-mayor of Animas City, and Nick Dramer, were standing with Woods near the courtroom when he said to them, "Here comes Mrs. Port Stockton's husband. Watch him and you will see him feel for his gun when he sees me."

They did as he suggested, and sure enough the moment Joel Estes lay eyes on George he slid his hand inside his coat for his Colt shoved in his waistband.

"Joel and Milt both have made threats to kill me," he emphasized as they watched.

Woods, ironically that morning on his way to the courthouse, met Milt on the street who instantly placed his hand on his revolver. George wordlessly opened his coat to show he was unarmed, and proceeded around him.

After his court hearing Woods dropped into Kincaid's Pacific Slope Saloon for a drink. At the end of the bar stood Milt Buchanan who immediately straightened upon seeing him. George ignored him and ordered a beer. While he was taking a sip Milt stepped over and said, "George, I'd like a word with you." In his hand against his thigh was a hunting knife with a five-inch blade. "Let's you and me step in the back room."

"I've got nothing to say to you, Milt. I've got no business with you at all."

Buchanan then turned to Kincaid, the proprietor who was tending bar, and loudly made the complaint, "I wanted to talk to Woods, but he refused! You saw it!"

George then wisely left the establishment, got a gun, and unwisely reentered the saloon. Walking the length of the bar he passed Milt who was belaboring the issue with customers.

"He won't talk to me," complained Milt. "And he's making threats!"

Woods sat at a table with Eber Smith and said, "Let's play a game of Cribbage."

"George," implored Smith in a whisper, motioning with his head. "Go on out the back door. Do it now, please."

But Woods was way beyond following intelligent instruction. He sat quietly attentive, an actor awaiting his next cue. He had not long to wait.

"There sits a man who won't talk to me," sounded Milt's mocking voice above the soft riffle of the deck.

Calmly, and past the point of no return, George rose from his seat and said loud enough for Buchanan to hear, "I'll talk to you now."

Milt heard and looked over as George turned with drawn weapon and walked toward the bar.

As he raised the gun Milt cried out in alarm, "I'm not armed!" George squeezed off a hasty shot which missed. The bullet broke a glass in a patron's hand next to Milt and went on to shatter the bar mirror. His second shot caught Milt square in the chest, felling him. On his back the shocked and wide-eyed Buchanan looked up at his assailant and said, "I am dead." To make certain, Woods pumped three more bullets into him. George then turned and walked out of the saloon. Deputy Charles O'Conner happened by when he heard the shots and was about to enter the building. Handing the Colt to the law, Woods said, "I have killed a man and I want to give myself up."

TWENTY FIVE

During his trial George wrote several letters to his aunt, Angeline Tucker. On 12 June he instructed her to "Have E. Brinkley to pay the 20.00 he owes me to Lizzie & Guy. Sutton owes me for my pistol, have him pay you for it to give to her." Labeling Ellen as black-hearted for breaking up his romance with Lizzie, he went on to say, "Jane (Emily) Estes is a virtuous woman, that I know, but she did not treat me right, although I cannot say anything against her, for she is a good woman, and I can forgive her for what she said against me."

Earlier in the letter he wrote, "I will write to you for the last time, for I have got to die soon . . . it is hard to think of dying to some, but it is not for me, for I have nothing to live for, since I lost my loved one who is so dear to me. Oh, how I would like to see her before I die! It would be such a relief to me. But it is impossible for me to see the one that I loved better than myself, for I sent for her father to come and see me so that I could get to see her, thinking he could not refuse me the privilege under the circumstances, but he positively refused to do, which I do not think was right, for you know I never mistreated him in all my life, with all the mistreatment he has shown me, because I loved his girl, whom I could not help loving after once seeing, Aunt Ange. I do blame her father for telling people that he did not give me the girl, for you know that he gave her and the ranch to me, and I went and worked one day on the house when Ellen's letter broke it up by stating obscene lies, saying that I lived with a bad woman when everybody knows that she is the only one that I had, thinking she was a good woman, but they are mistaken for she will do anything to flirt with N. C. Caldwell (sic) and to keep up appearance (sic) . . . Aunt Angie, she must have a terrible black heart to do as she does, and then meet people with the smile she does (sic)."

The jury found George Napoleon Woods guilty of deliberate and premeditated murder, and the execution date was set for 23 June 1882. Before an audience of about 300, Woods was hanged shortly before noon exactly one month after his own execution of Milt Buchanan. A few minutes before his descent he was converted and baptized by Pastor M. C. Brennen. Yet reportedly, his last words on the scaffold to the presiding hangman, Sheriff Barney Watson, were that "he regretted not killing Joel Estes."

Seeing Bill Valliant in the pressing crowd before him he raised his shackled fists above his head, gesturing desperately from his podium, and shouted, "Tell them, Bill, tell them! I have been unfairly branded, used and brtrayed! An unsatisfied exit, this! I was casting bread upon the waters! Oh, Bill, tell them my tale! Farewell!"

Scattered raucous laughter rent the crowd while impatient hands gripped and strapped his body. As his head was encased in a black hood the world around him vanished. In moments the trap swung open and he felt himself shooting weightlessly downward, his gut experiencing its last thrill. His body jerked at the bottom of the fall with a brutal crack he never felt or heard, leaving him breathless, thoughtless and lifeless. He was left now with the dubious distinction of being the only man to be legally hanged in La Plata County. The prosecuting attorney was Nathaniel Colbert Coldwell.

CODA

Three days after George Woods swung, Amanda Ellen Stockton married Nathaniel C. Coldwell. Following their marriage Ellen gave birth to two more children, Colbert in 1883 and Julia in 1885. Sometime after the birth of Julia, probably in 1886, the Coldwell family moved to Fresno, California, where Nathaniel continued his profession. The shift was reportedly made after a friend in Fresno, a judge, suggested strongly there was plenty of opportunities there for a lawyer. The added impetus may also have been a natural and pressing desire for both to leave behind and bury the memories of Durango and Ellen's early marriage to outlaw Ike Stockton. Too, perhaps Nathaniel was more than ready to leave. On 4 March 1884 he was arrested in Durango for using offensive language and carrying concealed weapons. Gossip may have ignited his fury.

Emily and Joel Estes Jr. birthed a pair of sons, Cleveland in 1884, and James in 1886, making a total of eleven children in the combined brood. After Emily died in 1893, Joel married Sarah E. Shannon in 1896 in Farmington, his third marriage. Sadly, Joel's two boys were said to have been, "not bright in mind," and were often recipients of cruel jokes. Cleveland, 32, working at a cattle ranch in the southeast corner of Utah, in a quarrel over a coat during breakfast on 21 November 1916, shot his young antagonist, Dick Granath, to death. The *Mancos Times-Tribune* of Colorado on 24 November 1916 carried the story.

FATAL SHOOTING OUT IN UTAH

"A fatal shooting took place out on Montezuma Creek, in the east edge of Utah, on Tuesday as the result of a quarrel which arose between two men over a coat. Dick Granath, a young Mexican, was killed. He was shot through from side to side just below the arm pits and died instantly. He was shot by Cleve, known as "Hunk," Estes, a brother to Mrs. James Nash. Estes is not bright and he was often made the victim of practical jokes which were cruel and wrong, and it is thought that perhaps one of those jokes was carried a little too far as often happens in such cases.

"Granath leaves a young wife but no children. Both men live about Dolores. Estes escaped and had not been caught at last report."

A week later, on 1 December, the paper continued.

"Cleve Estes, who last week shot and killed Dick Granath out on the edge of Utah, acting on the advice of friends, went up to Montezuma and surrendered. It was probably the first time the poor fellow ever had any real good friendly advise. Hugh Rentz was at the cow camp when the shooting took place and went with Estes to Monticello. All sorts of stories are rife in regard to the shooting." Estes was sentenced to 15 years for murder in the second degree, and incarcerated in the Utah State prison. After petitioned by family and many friends who went to bat for him, feeling the sentence was too harsh, he was paroled about 1920, then freed.

In late 1925 in La Plata County, Colorado, Cleveland was convicted for "indecent liberties with children," and given two to three years in the Colorado State Penitentiary. He was described as, "42, 5-6, 146 pounds, medium complexion, blue eyes, grey hair."

In1895, according to one account, Port and Emily's youngest daughter Carrie, nine months shy of her 16th year, had the chore of delivering meals to prisoners at the Animas City hoosegow, her stepfather Joel Estes Jr. reportedly the town deputy. One of the prisoners, horse thief Acel Durias "Acy" Wilmot, 23, caught her fancy, titillating her with tales of the bank robbers he led. As a result, on 7 May Carrie filched a pair of saddle horses from her step-dad's stock, upon which the two eloped. Riding off to Durango, one mile south, they applied for a marriage license. But something occurred which caused them to abort their plans, and the licence was, "Returned May 9,1895 without being used." They then hastened to Farmington, New Mexico where they wed on 2 June. After this Carrie was known as "Essie May Wilmot." Whose idea it was for the name alteration is unknown, but if it was for an attempt at invisibility, or to secrete her marriage, it was a poor one, for to find Carrie one had but to find Acel Wilmot on the records.

Their first child, Grace Maud, was born in Oklahoma in 1902, indicating how far the couple had fled from Colorado.

But by1910 they had gravitated back to Colorado, to the prosperous village of Glendale, Fremont County, about 200 crow-flight miles northeast of Durango, and 11 miles west of Pueblo. In 1911 the community would consolidate itself with Penrose. It was mainly a farming district, and early on quite thriving, where Acy may have tried farming for a time. By this time the couple had three children; Grace 10, George 7 and Howard 5. Acel is now "Asahal D. Miland," and Carrie, "May E. Miland." Essie's father for some reason was listed on the census as "Stockton Miland." They no doubt were still laying low, Carrie from her irate step-father, and Acy from his horse-theft charges.

By 1916 another move took them farther north to Utah, where on 15 May, Acy D. Wilmot was charged, convicted and sentenced for larceny in Davis County, Utah for "100 days or $100." On 7 July Acy filed for a pardon, claiming to have paid $1,800 cash, plus thereafter incarcerated for ten days.

During this imbroglio Grace Maud, the Wilmot's 18-year-old daughter, married Edward Parks Johnson, 36, on 26 February 1916. She was his second wife. Johnson's previous ten years were spent in and out of the jails of Nevada and Utah for the crimes of larceny and forgery. Where, when or how he and Acy met is unknown, but it is certain it was through their common criminal milieu. Yet, no evidence has surfaced whether the two had ever combined their low talents in any illegal undertaking. But strangely, on Acy's application for the pardon mentioned earlier, "Edward Johnson: Salt Lake City", appears to have signed on as a character witness.

In 1920, "Ashal" D. Wilmot, 47, and Essie May Wilmot, 40, are living in Pine Grove, Santa Barbara County, California. With them are their two sons, Howard D., 14, and Johnny C., 8. Their daughter Grace Maud Johnson, 20, is also present with her two children, Genoa M.,

2, and Edward Johnson, newly born. Grace's husband Edward Parks Johnson is absent. Divorcing, he married twice more, dying in 1946.

In 1930 Grace Maud, 28, and her second husband, Lewis L. Aker, 34, are in Calexico, Imperial County, California, where he works as a truck farmer. With them are their five children, three Johnsons and two Akers. At this time also present were Acy and Essie—but living apart, Acy in Holtville and Essie in Calexico. While living with Grace and working as a laundress, Essie claimed she was a widow. Acy, 20 miles north in Holtville, labored in a gravel pit and said he was married. If their marriage had finally played out its string, or if it was just another one of those bumps on the road of romance, it isn't known.

Essie May Wilmot, nee Carrie Stockton, born 21 September 1879 in Otero, New Mexico, died 25 September 1940 in Los Angeles, California. She was 61. Asel Durias Wilmot, born 6 November 1872 in Camden, Missouri, also died in Los Angeles, on 19 March 1954, seven days following a surgical operation. He was 81. He was attended by his daughter, Grace Aker

The Port Stocktons' oldest daughter, Sarah Ellen, after one known marriage to A. B. Johnson in Durango 29 May 1891, and perhaps eight children over the years, died at 59 in Brea, California in 1931. Of her Johnson marriage she lost a pair of twins at 8 months, and a son, Walt, at 8 years. In her Sheeran relationship she birthed a son and 3 daughters. Her son Lester was reportedly lynched at 15 or 16 for stealing a horse.

Their second daughter, Mary Jane, 24 in 1900, was living in Hermosa, Colorado with Jason Hyett, 27. Her death date is unknown, but she was buried in the Animas City Cemetery to the right of her uncle, Isaac Thomas Stockton. Her stone has since mysteriously fled the graveyard.

In Fresno in 1888 Ellen Coldwell birthed a daughter, Nora, and in 1890 a son, Cedric. The Coldwells occasionally experienced rocky times, and in 1894 both engineered a determined and swift divorce. It was granted "all in a small part of the day," as described in the *Fresno Weekly Republican* of 5 October. Ellen filed on the grounds of cruelty, claiming that Nathaniel refused Ellen's relations to visit her home. It appears to have evolved mainly over daughter Delilah, now 20. Guy was 14. The young woman was not only forbidden in the home, but Nathaniel further demanded she give up her employment at a Fresno business before allowed readmittance. Delilah had moved out and gone to work, leaving her father angered. He claimed it was a humiliation to him for her to have a job, that her place was in the home until she married. Ellen sided with her daughter. Pointedly, Nathaniel never did adopt Ellen's two offspring by Ike Stockton, so it is possible filial resentment was involved, for rumors spoke of strained relations between the father and his two step-children.

The divorce was instantly granted, with Ellen given custody of the children as she requested. On the day before the divorce Nathaniel had deeded to his wife a pair of lots in Fresno.

The *Republican* also commented that five years previous he had been unjustly associated with a Mrs. Sarah Althea Terry, "a woman whose mission on earth seemed to cause misery in the homes of men." Sarah Terry was a lovely siren of grand romantic presence who carried her own stigmata of personal agonies, enough to spend her last 35 years in an insane asylum, mind-broken and shattered. Nathaniel always denied the allegations, and the paper described him as most unhappy and embittered following the divorce. Whether the assertions were true or false, the circulating stories may have added a slow burn to his wife's imagination over the years.

Yet, not two weeks later, the *Republican* announced on 12 October in a banner column that the two had "HAPPILY REUNITED," and remarried. After the ceremony a collection of friends gathered at the parlor of the Emanuel Baptist Church for a congratulatory party. Whatever the difficulties, all seems to have been satisfactorily smoothed over.

Delilah Coldwell married Louis Detoy in 1897, who was born in France in 1873. The pair, after living in San Francisco with Ellen and Nathaniel for a time, settled in Santa Cruz for the rest of their lives. They had four children, a boy and three girls. Louis died in 1951 at 77, and Delilah in 1963 at 88.

By 1920 Ike's 40-year-old son Guy was a wealthy success as a real estate broker in Fresno. Earlier, on 4 November 1905 he married Ivah Winifred Lawrence, with whom they had two sons, Frank "Robin" Robinson and Norman Grant. But the marriage didn't hold. Divorcing amicably, they each took a son to raise, Guy opting for Robin. On 31 December 1914 he wed Florence Brocklebank. In 1926 he ran for mayor, but was defeated. Later, a casualty of the economic crash of the 1930s, he was left destitute and devastated, dying in 1932. He was 52.

Another of the Coldwell clan who entered the real estate profession was Colbert, Nathaniel and Ellen's oldest son. After viewing the devastating aftermath of the San Francisco earthquake of 1906, the 23-year-old agent founded a company of his own. Becoming enormously prosperous, in 1914 he took in a full-time partner, Benjamin Arthur Banker, and together they formed the Coldwell Banker Real Estate Association.

Nathaniel Colbert Coldwell died 30 May 1914, followed by his wife Amanda Ellen ten years later on 7 January 1924. He was 60; she 66, born in 1854 in Texas.

Charles Adams Jones (1861-1934), owner and editor of Rico's *Dolores News* from 1880 to 1886, and an early defender of Ike and his gang of "crusaders," soon discovered what a fool he had been. Years later he confessed, "I had been trying to help men who were in the main most untrustworthy." He pleaded his youth, and that life in the state at that time was raw. "I was supporting (them) in every way for the reasons I believed them seriously imposed upon and wholly right in fighting for property rights. But it drew me into a vortex where I was perilously near ruin."

And last but not least, as of this writing, Pamela Selway Birmingham, a descendent of William Porter Stockton, is a real estate broker in Seaside, Oregon.

An Added Curiosity

Just moments before being shot, after Ike Stockton left Marion Galbreath at the wagon and walked down the street alone, a local businessman, J. K. Mills, happened on the scene. He knew Ike and saw him strolling a short distance away. But with Ike he saw another man, whom to Mills was a stranger. After a few moments Stockton and his companion turned a corner and disappeared. To quote the *Dolores News:*

> *Mr. J. K. Mills, of this city, is a spiritualist, but not a medium. He is a prominent businessman, a man of veracity, and commands the respect of his friends and acquaintances. The following is Mr. Mills' experience as related by himself:*
>
> *Just before the arrest and shooting of Ike Stockton, Mr. Mills, as he states, saw him coming along H Street in company with another man, who was an entire stranger to Mr. Mills. A moment later the arrest was made, the shooting was done, and the second man had vanished. No one else, as far as Mr. Mills could learn by the most diligent inquiry, saw the second man, and consequently no one could tell who he was. Somewhat later Mr. Mills saw a picture of Bert Wilkinson, the man who Ike Stockton betrayed to his death but a few weeks since, and to his utter astonishment he said that he was the man he had seen in the vision it undoubtedly was, as no such person was with Stockton at the time.*
>
> *Whether this was a hallucination or spectre, who shall say? We tell the tale as told to us by Mr. Mills himself, whom everyone in Durango knows, and leave our readers to draw their own inferences. Mr. Mills states that he was laboring under no excitement, that he of course had no*

knowledge of the arrest, and that he did not know who the man was until Wilkinson's picture. Let who will or can account for the phenomenon.

So it seems the lynch mob got its wish when it shouted, "Go to hell with Bert Wilkinson!" It appears Bert made a special trip to collect Ike to personally escort him downstairs.

Acknowledgments

I especially wish to thank the following individuals for their time and kindness in sharing photographs, genealogical data, family and historical information, and general lore for this work:

Pam Birmingham, Bob and Gail Kaufmann, Reba Beebe Luzar, Mike Maddox, Avis Moore, Frederick Nolan, Julie Pickett, John Pierson, Monte Pruett, Rusty Salmon, Carol Wahl, and Roxie.